MY BEST FRIEND IS A VIRAL DANCING ZOMBIE

KARIN ADAMS

James Lorimer & Company Ltd., Publishers
Toronto

James Lorimer & Company Ltd., Publishers acknowledges the support of
the Ontario Arts Council (OAC), an agency of the Government of Ontario,
which in 2015-16 funded 1,676 individual artists and 1,125 organizations in
209 communities across Ontario for a total of $50.5 million. We acknowledge
the support of the Canada Council for the Arts, which last year invested $153
million to bring the arts to Canadians throughout the country. This project has
been made possible in part by the Government of Canada and with the support
of the Ontario Media Development Corporation.

Cover design: Tyler Cleroux
Cover and interior images: Shutterstock

978-1-4594-1130-2
eBook also available 978-1-4594-1128-9

Cataloguing data available from Library and Archives Canada.

Published by:
James Lorimer & Company Ltd.,
Publishers
117 Peter Street, Suite 304
Toronto, ON, Canada
M5V 0M3
www.lorimer.ca

Distributed by:
Lerner Publishing Services
1251 Washington Ave N
Minneapolis, MN, USA
55401
www.lernerbooks.com

Printed and bound in Canada.
Manufactured by Friesens Corporation in Altona, Manitoba, Canada in
December 2016.
Job #228984

For Matthew

#1
Rise of the mighty Lizard Beast

Online movie Festival — coming soon!

Riley Foster stared at the bright green words on the classroom whiteboard. They leaped out at him like a 3D movie action scene. Some of Riley's grade five classmates shuffled past him. "Cool," "Neat," "Looks fun," they mumbled and then moved on. But Riley stayed in front of the board as though his feet were glued to the carpet. His backpack slid from his shoulder and thudded to the floor.

"Hey, Riley. You dropped your . . . *whoa*!" It was Riley's best friend, Finn Sawchuk. Finn looked at the board with the same dazed look on his face as Riley's.

"*Do you think — ?*" Finn began to whisper to Riley. The morning bell broke in. They'd have to wait until after "O Canada" for more information.

Throughout the anthem and the morning announcements, Riley's brain was on fire. He was sure that their teacher, Mr. Kim, would be asking them to make their own movies. His class had spent the last couple of weeks on stop-motion animation using the classroom laptops. But "online movie festival"? Was it some sort of contest? Riley certainly hoped so. He'd been making animated videos for years. He'd even won first prize in a short film contest last July for Canada Day. His name and picture had been in the newspaper. Maybe this time he'd get on TV. . .

Finally Mr. Kim gathered the class on the carpet by the whiteboard. "All right, people," he said. "Over the next few weeks, you're going to be making your own original movies. You can use live action, stop-motion or a combination."

Riley and Finn, sitting side by side, looked at each other and did a mini fist pump.

"And to share all your hard work and creativity, I'll be posting your movies on our class blog," Mr. Kim continued. "It will be our very own online movie festival, going live on March 22. You can invite your family and friends to watch the movies and leave comments."

Jasmine Santos raised her hand. "Even if some of your family lives in the Philippines?" she asked. She was always talking about her cousins who lived there.

"Well, it's online, so yes," Mr. Kim said. "I guess technically we can call it an international movie festival."

Riley sure liked the sound of that! "Will there be awards?" he asked, leaning forward.

"Ooh . . . good idea, Riley," said Jasmine. She pushed a strand of long black hair off her face and smiled at him. He felt his cheeks turn suddenly warm. "If it's a festival, we *have* to have awards, Mr. Kim."

"Like Best Story," Jasmine's friend Claire suggested.

"Or Best Special Effects," added Navdeep.

"How about Most Hilarious?" offered Finn.

"Best Picture!" Riley said, a big grin spreading across his face.

"Okay — these are good ideas," said Mr. Kim. "We'll brainstorm a complete list later. We'll also have to plan a way for every film to get an award for what it did best." That was just fine with Riley. He could smell a Best Picture victory in his future.

"Also, keep in mind that our festival isn't just about awards. It's about getting creative and using some of your new animation skills."

New for some of us, thought Riley.

"And mostly, it's about collaboration," Mr. Kim continued. "I want to see in each project how you worked together as a team. You can even work with other groups and help each other. In the end, it should be very clear that your movie was a team effort."

"Can we pick our own groups?" asked Jasmine. She linked arms with Claire and Arusha.

"Yes," said Mr. Kim. "But no more than three per team. And let's choose *wisely*, people." Riley was pretty sure that Mr. Kim was looking at Paulo and Vijay. (The two boys were fooling around at the far edge of the carpet.)

Meanwhile, Riley and Finn locked eyes and nodded. Of course they'd work together — they always did. In fact, Riley and Finn were already making an action-packed film at Riley's place after school. They called it *Lizard Beast versus the Zombie Horde*. It starred Riley's pet bearded dragon named Slow-Mo and a set of (zombified) soldier action figures.

"Can our movies be about anything?" someone asked.

"As long as you're using your own original ideas," said Mr. Kim. "Nothing from movies, books or video games."

A few shoulders drooped, but Riley and Finn high-fived. *Lizard Beast* was absolutely original.

Who else in the class was going to have a real, live lizard mixed in with animation?

"And keep it *appropriate* for school," added Mr. Kim. This time, the teacher was *definitely* looking at Paulo and Vijay, who were miming ninja moves on each other. "You can have *conflict*, but no senseless violence or gross-out stuff."

We can work around that, Riley thought. They would probably have to tone down some of their zombie swarm scenes, but it would be worth it.

Mr. Kim explained a few more details about the project, like how they'd have a few periods per week to work on their movies and how there were enough digital cameras available for all the groups. Part of Riley's brain was listening to the details. The other part was busy planning new movie scenes: Lizard Beast chasing the Zombie Horde through a dark jungle . . . zombies learning to fly . . .

"One last thing," said Mr. Kim. "Our first deadline will

be March 15." He pointed to the class calendar. "This will be our 'sneak preview.' That means everyone will show a short clip from their movies to the class. We'll give each other feedback to improve the final versions for the festival."

"We'll give the class a sneak preview" — Riley whispered to Finn — "*of our epic awesomeness!*" They high-fived again.

As the class headed back to their desks, Riley turned to Finn. "My place after school?" he asked.

★ ★ ★

On the ride home from school, Riley and Finn talked nonstop about their movie.

"We'll make Lizard Island out of pillows and blankets," said Riley. "Good thing my living room carpet looks like sand . . ."

"I'll make a soundtrack on your keyboard," said Finn. "And some homemade sound effects . . ."

Their ideas were flowing like molten lava from an erupting volcano.

Riley grabbed his movie notebook from his

backpack. He turned to a fresh page to write everything down. He wasn't going to let a single thought slip away!

"Lizard Beast Versus The Zombie Horde" A Stop-Motion Action Blockbuster Script!

Written, Animated, Filmed and Directed by Riley Foster

Music and Sound Effects by Finn Sawchuk

The Cast:

Riley as Rocket

Finn as Flapjack

Slow-Mo the bearded dragon as Lizard Beast (voice by Finn or Riley)

Riley and Finn as Various Zombies

The Main Movie Idea:

Lizard Beast's private island is under attack from an army of Special Ops soldiers who have turned into zombies. Two soldiers — with the code names "Rocket" and "Flapjack" — are immune to the zombie virus. They become Lizard Beast's allies. The three best friends must work together to defeat the Zombie Horde . . . *but time is running out!*

#2
Deleted Scenes

"He's not moving," said Finn. He tapped the glass of the lizard enclosure with his fingernail. "*HELLOOOOO* in there! . . . *Sllllloooow-Mo* . . ."

"That's not going to work," said Riley from behind the tripod in his living room. He was recording video footage with his digital camera. For the past fifteen minutes, he'd been trying to film Slow-Mo doing something — *anything!* — as Lizard Beast. Riley knew he could just take still pictures and "animate" them. But the whole point of using Slow-Mo in their movie was to blend animation with a real, live lizard.

"I'll try feeding him again," said Finn.

"Don't. I think he's full," Riley protested. But Finn had already opened the glass doors to Slow-Mo's vivarium. Finn loved fooling around with Slow-Mo whenever he came over. He couldn't have any pets in his apartment, so he made up for it at Riley's place. Finn grabbed a piece of spinach from the food bowl and dangled it in front of the lizard's mouth.

"Forget Slow-Mo for now. Let's do a different scene," said Riley.

"I know!" Finn bounded toward Riley's mini electric keyboard. "How about we work on the soundtrack?" Finn pressed a button and then a few keys.

The only thing Finn loved more than Slow-Mo was messing around on Riley's keyboard. He set the instrument to his favourite sound: stardust. As he played a few notes, a sound like chimes in a breeze filled the air. It made Riley picture a faraway ice planet.

"Lizard Beast lives on a tropical island,

Finn," said Riley. "We need music that sounds
. . . *sweatier*."

"No problem!" said Finn. He stuck his hand
through the neck of his T-shirt and cupped it
under his armpit. "Sweaty enough for you?" he
asked as he flapped his arm to make squawking
sounds.

Riley powered down the camera and plopped
himself beside the coffee table. He liked working with Finn. Sometimes he even liked
getting carried away with Finn's goofi-
ness. But now, they had to *focus*. How
else would they show the class their epic
movie-making skills?

"We can't really do the music
until we finish the scenes," said Riley.
He grabbed his movie notebook and
opened to a page filled with bright green
sticky notes. On each note, he'd sketched the
main action for a scene they were planning to
film. Riley had learned the storyboard tech-
nique at animation camp.

"How about this one?" Riley said, pointing

to the second sticky from the left. Finn, still focused on the keyboard, didn't answer. He was too busy checking out a sound called angry cat. Whenever Finn played a note, it sounded as though someone had stepped on a cat's tail.

"FINN!" Riley shouted over the screechy noise. Finn stopped and looked up. He left the keyboard and flopped down beside Riley.

"Is this the scene where Rocket and Flapjack are on the beach?" Finn asked.

"Yeah — right before they meet Lizard Beast for the first time," said Riley. "Let's get our dudes."

Riley and Finn reached into the shoebox full of old action figures. Of course, they'd chosen the ones who looked like themselves to star in their movie. Riley's soldier — Rocket — was black and had a buzzed hairdo just like Riley, although he didn't have Riley's glasses. Finn's guy — Flapjack — was white with wavy red-dish-blond hair like him, but none of Finn's freckles. (Of course, neither Riley nor Finn had a manly beard or super-ripped muscles, but that was beside the point.)

Riley and Finn placed Rocket and Flapjack on the beige living room carpet (a.k.a. the sandy island beach). Behind them were a couple of cushions covered by a worn grey blanket (a.k.a. mountains on the island). Riley rearranged the sheet of shiny blue wrapping paper (a.k.a. the tropical sea) so it looked as though it rippled with waves.

"There's a tidal wave sound on the keyboard," Finn pointed out.

"Great," said Riley. "We'll add it in later." He stood up slowly and tiptoed back to the tripod, trying not to disturb a thing. He looked through the camera, moving it to exactly the right angle.

"Don't bounce!" Riley warned Finn, who was heading for Slow-Mo's vivarium. Any extra movement would throw off the stop-motion effect.

"I'm just walking," Finn insisted.

"Well, do it less bouncily. You're jiggling the tripod."

When the camera was finally

set up just right, Riley began taking pictures. Between shots, he'd rush over to the set, move Rocket's arm up by a millimetre, or turn Flapjack's head slightly to the left. The movements had to be teeny-tiny so that Riley could create seamless stop-motion action.

"Nooo!" Riley smacked his forehead as a

mountain fell over for the tenth time in a row.

"Can I do something yet?" asked Finn.

"Just a minute," said Riley. "ARGH! All this footage is *useless*."

"This scene's kind of boring anyway," Finn said. "Let's film the Zombie Horde instead." He went back to the shoebox and grabbed a handful of extra action figures.

"Hello — who are you?" With a silly grin, Finn pulled out an old plastic princess figure with long black hair and a green dress. Someone had added bright pink lips with a marker.

"That's just Kennedy's old thing," said Riley. Kennedy was his fourteen-year-old sister. "It must have gotten mixed up with the action figures."

With the princess still in hand, Finn grabbed Rocket off the floor. He hit the video record button on the camera.

"Finn — what are you . . ." Riley began. But it was too late.

"Ooh! Riley 'Rocket' Foster! Is that really you?" Finn was waving the princess doll in front of the camera and talking in his girliest voice. "Don't you recognize me? It's Jasmine Santos from Mr. Kim's grade five class. You have *soooo* many muscles now! Do you want to go out with me?"

"Hey — shut that off!" Riley said, lunging for the camera. Riley knew that Finn knew that he kind of, sort of liked Jasmine.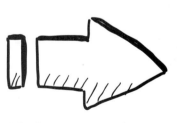

But Finn blocked Riley with his arm and kept going. He waved Rocket in front of the camera lens. "I'd love to take you on a date, Jasmine," Finn said with a manly grunt. "Good thing we're on this romantic island."

Riley managed to reach the off button. He glared at Finn.

"What? It was just for fun," said Finn, snickering. Then suddenly, the goofy grin on his face straightened out. "Wait a minute . . . we should totally have deleted scenes!"

"Deleted scenes?"

Finn dropped the action figures and grabbed Riley's movie notebook. He flipped to a fresh page. "You know — like they sometimes show at the end of movies. When the actors' names come up," Finn explained.

"You mean the credits?" Riley said.

"Right — the credits! You know how they play the goof-up scenes that got cut out from the movie? Where the actors laugh during their lines, or say the wrong thing, or get hit in the face with something by accident . . ."

Riley nodded his head. He saw where

Finn was going with this. He liked it! "So whenever *we* goof up a scene," Riley said, "we should keep it to play at the end of our film."

"Right!" said Finn. He scrawled his new idea into the notebook with his uneven, messy printing.

"I bet no one else will think of it," said Riley. "Plus, it's proof that we actually did some editing." Mr. Kim was big on editing. Finn's deleted scenes could really be another Best Picture advantage.

Finn looked up, his eyes wide. "I know what to do for our first deleted scene!"

"We are NOT using the princess thing," Riley said firmly. "Wait — what do you mean an *idea*? I thought the deleted scenes are just our movie mess-ups."

"We can plan some of them. They do that in real movies," said Finn. "Why not? We can come up with some super-funny stuff. Do you have any construction paper and tape?" Clearly Finn had an idea.

"Uh, yeah. In the closet in the front hall. But remember that stop-motion takes forever. We can't spend *all* of our time making extra scenes just for fun."

"What about scissors?"

"Same place. But Finn, didn't you hear me?" Riley asked. Finn had a habit of zoning out sometimes.

"Yeah, yeah. Animation takes time. But not all the deleted scenes have to be animated." Finn headed for the front hall. "We can just wave the figures around and give them funny voices. It'll be hilarious!"

Riley was about to protest when he noticed another cushion mountain fall over on the set. It smothered Flapjack. Riley sprang to his feet and followed Finn to the supply closet.

At least we'll get something done today, thought Riley. *Even if it's just a deleted scene.*

DELETED SCENE: "Facial Hair Contest"

Riley as Rocket
Finn as Flapjack
Slow-Mo as Lizard Beast

Close-up of Flapjack and Rocket arguing.

FLAPJACK: **My** beard is the manliest-*est*.

ROCKET: Ha! You call that a beard? I have WAY more facial hair than you.

FLAPJACK: Oh yeah? Check this out.

Flapjack goes out of the camera's view. Flapjack returns half a second later. He is now wearing a huge stick-on paper moustache that curls up at both ends.

ROCKET: Ha! That's nothing. Watch this!

Rocket goes out of view. Rocket returns moments later wearing a stuck-on paper beard. The beard is longer than his body.

FLAPJACK: Wait a minute. We've both been beat. Look!

The camera turns toward Lizard Beast. Zoom in on the bearded dragon's impressive spiky. scaly beard. (Slow-Mo puffs it out.)

In the background. Rocket and Flapjack grumble about their own unmanly beards.

#3
Yeesh — Drama!

"Boys — do you have to be so close to the TV?" said Riley's dad from his big, reclining leather chair. "I can barely see the game."

Finn and Riley, plus Riley's family, were in the living room after dinner. The big hockey game was on TV. The hometown Knights were playing the Eagles. But Riley and Finn were only half-watching. They were busy gathering footage for their movie.

"But this corner has the best lighting," Riley explained. He aimed the camera toward Slow-Mo. The lizard was out of his vivarium and crawling around on the living room carpet.

"Yeah, Dad," grumbled Riley's sister, Kennedy. She was sitting on the couch texting her friends. "Don't mess up their Hollywood *masterpiece*."

Riley shot Kennedy a greasy look.

"Remember to wash up when you're finished playing with Slow-Mo," said Riley's mom. She was on the couch reading a book on her tablet.

"*With soap*," added Riley's dad.

"We're not *playing*," Riley protested.

"Are we still going to give Slow-Mo a bath?" Finn asked Riley.

"Later. I still need to get a good shot of . . ."

"*Go, go, GO!*" Riley's dad suddenly cried. He leaned forward in his chair. Riley's mom lowered her tablet to her lap and shouted, "SHOOT THE PUCK!" Everyone stared as the Knights captain, Beau Thomas, glided toward the Eagles net. Even Riley put down his camera.

Beau Thomas wound up with his stick.

He took a shot.

The puck sped toward the goalie. And then . . .

"*Awww!*" Everyone groaned. The puck sailed wide of the net — no goal!

"The Knights just can't get a break these days," said Riley's dad.

"No luck," Riley's mom agreed. Just then, her tablet binged with an incoming message. "Hey, Blake," she said to Riley's dad. "It's Desmond. They can't make it to the game Saturday afternoon. Want the extra tickets?" Riley's family had two of their own season tickets to the Knights games. Plus they always got first shot at Uncle Desmond's seats when he and Aunt Sherie were busy.

"Ooh!" Kennedy squealed as she jumped up in her seat. "Let me go this time! I want to take Dahlia. We have *the best* plan to win Leon Courage tickets!"

"You mean for his I'm So In 2U Tour?" Riley turned to face his sister, fluttering his eyelashes. He and Finn laughed. They were always joking about the pop idol from Saskatoon with his super-skinny pants and weird poufy hair. For some reason, all the girls in the universe seemed to be in love with him.

"That guy is so fake," said Riley.

"Leon Courage is so *not* fake," Kennedy said. "He's *amazing*!"

Finn poked Riley. He clutched his stomach and pretended to throw up. Riley smirked.

Kennedy kept babbling: "His tour looks *amazing*. And Dahlia and I have an *amazing* plan to win tickets."

"Sweetie . . ." Riley's mom tried to interrupt.

"Remember the Knights game when they gave free concert tickets to those two girls who danced to his song? They weren't even *good*. So I said to Dahlia, 'Hey, we could totally do that.' So that's our plan," said Kennedy, her pink-streaked corkscrew curls bouncing.

"You're going to go to the game and dance really bad?" asked Finn.

"*No*. We're going to bring a *huge* sign with Leon Courage's face on it. We'll dress up like the dancers in his new video —"

"You mean those weird robot things?" Riley said. Finn jumped to his feet. He started doing jerky robot dance moves just like Leon Courage in his latest video, "Luv U Thru Time." Riley snickered as he pictured Finn wearing the same silver face paint and tinfoil clothes.

"They're not *robots*. The song is about the *future* and undying love," Kennedy said.

"I. AM. FROM. THE. FUTURE," Finn said, waving his arms stiffly.

Kennedy grabbed a cushion, threatening to clobber Riley and Finn with it. But before she could, her mom said, "Kennedy, you have your ringette tournament Saturday. Remember?"

Kennedy lowered the cushion. She deflated into the couch like an old party balloon.

"Riley and I will go this time,"

said Riley's dad. "Finn, do you think you and your dad could join us?"

Finn's jaw dropped. "Really?" he asked.

"Sure. Unless Brian's working . . ."

Finn shook his head. "No, not this Saturday. But I bet he'd book it off anyway. We've never been to a Knights game!"

"Really?" said Riley, surprised. He'd been to eight games already just that season.

"Riley got to go last time," Kennedy pointed out.

"It's not about that. You're busy Saturday. You can go to the next game."

Kennedy slumped farther down. "The concert will be over by then. This is my last chance to win Leon Courage tickets . . . WAIT!" Kennedy suddenly shot back up. "Maybe YOU guys can get on camera and win the tickets! Riley can hold the sign, and Finn, you could dance — you seem to know all the moves."

Finn turned bright red.

"No way," Riley protested.

"We're not holding up your girly sign with Leon Courage on it. *Gross.*"

"Kennedy, you'll get another chance," said Riley's dad.

"No, I won't. I won't *ever* get to see Leon Courage!"

"Yeesh — *drama*!" Riley said, shaking his head.

Kennedy gave her brother a dark look. "Whatever," she muttered, and went back to her texting. "I hope your faces *break* the jumbo screen."

"This face?" Riley asked. He widened his eyes and opened his mouth, morphing into a hungry zombie. He drifted toward Kennedy, groaning and pawing at her head. But before Kennedy could bat him away, Riley stopped. Kennedy had given him a great idea.

"Finn — *we* should make a sign and bring it to the game!" Riley said.

"To cheer on the Knights?" Finn asked.

"No! For *Lizard Beast versus the Zombie*

Horde." Riley rubbed his hands together. "We can put the date of the movie festival on it. And the URL for the class blog! *Thousands* of people will see it up there."

"What if we went viral?" Finn said, catching on. "We could be *famous*!"

"Yeah, right," Kennedy murmured.

"We should dress up, too," Riley added, ignoring his sister. "To get the camera's attention."

"We could wear big, crazy clown wigs," said Finn. "Or those weird stocking things over our faces in the team colours —"

"No, we need to dress up like *zombies*," said Riley. "To go with our sign! We could have torn-up clothes and junky boots . . ."

"Make fake scars on our cheeks . . ."

"Yeah! Of course, we have to *act* like zombies, too . . . *arggggle-arghhhhh* . . ." Riley leaned his zombie face close to Kennedy. She nudged him away roughly with her foot.

"Ugh! Get away. You're such a weird little —"

"*All-righty!*" said Riley's mom with a clap of

her hands. She jumped to her feet. "How about that bath for Slow-Mo?"

DELETED SCENE: "(No) Costumes. Hair and Makeup"

WARNING: CONTAINS BRIEF LIZARD NUDITY

Riley as the cameraman
Finn as Slow-Mo's personal assistant
   (and the voice of Slow-Mo)
Slow-Mo as himself (voice by Finn)

Finn is bathing Slow-Mo* in the bathroom sink. (Riley's mom is an extra with no lines.)

RILEY: Well, here we are in Slow-Mo's dressing room. Our movie star is getting ready for the big screen with help from his personal assistant. Let's see if we can get any hair and makeup tips from the big star himself.

Zoom in on Slow-Mo in the water.
RILEY: Mr. Slow-Mo, what's your celebrity secret for getting handsome for the big screen?

SLOW-MO: EEK! What are you doing? Get out of here! Can't you see . . . I'M TOTALLY NAKED!!!

FINN: But you're always naked, sir. You're a lizard!

SLOW-MO: TURN THAT THING OFF!!!

RILEY: Yeesh — drama!

*Post-production special effects: Riley will add a digital Leon Courage hairdo onto Slow-Mo's head.

#4
Jumbo
Finn

URGENT TO-DO LIST:

MAKE HUGE MOVIE SIGN:
✓ Find BRIGHT poster paper for movie sign (check
  Mom's craft closet?)
✓ Write title and blog in MARKER with MASSIVE
  LETTERS (to show up on the jumbo screen)

ZOMBIE COSTUME:
✓ Find Dad's old camp shirt (add more rips)
✓ Get boots gross at recess (slushy, muddy snow by
  the monkey bars)
✓ Figure out how to do makeup zombie scars (use
Kennedy's eye liner?)

GO VIRAL

"Nice makeup," said the security guard at the entrance to the hockey arena. She waved her metal detector wand over Riley's outstretched arms. "Are you supposed to be some kind of monster?"

"Zombie," said Riley, scrunching his face. Beneath his glasses, he felt the thick purple makeup he'd painted around his eyes crinkle like parched earth. The fake scars and stitches on his cheeks were itching like crazy, too. Riley sure hoped *someone* realized what he was supposed to be.

"Cute," the guard mumbled, then shouted *"Next!"*

Riley picked up his bright yellow sign from the floor and stepped through the turnstile. His dad spotted Finn and his father near the gourmet hot dog stand. They waded through the jam-packed lobby toward them. Riley was extra careful not to bend his sign.

"Brian! Finn!" Riley's dad

called out, waving his arms.

Riley's jaw dropped. *What on earth was Finn wearing?*

"Hey, Riley — check me out!" Finn spun around to show off his "costume." He was dressed in super-skinny black pants and unlaced sneakers. He 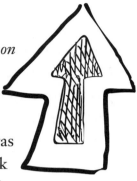 wore a bright red T-shirt and a shiny, fake-leather vest. His reddish hair was slicked back at the sides with hair gel. The front was swooped back into a pouf. He was wearing a touch of zombie makeup. But you could barely see it through his huge mirrored sunglasses! In fact, Finn kind of looked a lot like . . .

"You're an *undead* Leon Courage!" said Riley, horrified.

"Isn't it great?" Finn spun around again. Riley noticed that Finn had faked the skinny black pants. They were just his junky black sweatpants pinned tight with safety pins.

"What are you doing? This wasn't our plan," Riley said.

"It's even better!" said Finn. "Remember how Kennedy said they're looking for Leon Courage fans in the crowd?"

"But we don't want tickets to his dumb concert. We want our *movie* to go viral!"

"Trust me," Finn insisted. "Zombie Courage will get us on the jumbo screen."

Riley looked Finn up and down, from the top of his poufed hairdo to the silver glitter he'd stuck to his undone shoes. "You know *way* too much about Leon Courage, Finn," he grumbled, but then he decided to drop it. Maybe Finn's costume would help them get noticed.

"At least take off the sunglasses so you can see the game," said Riley.

"Fine," Finn agreed. He tucked his glasses into his vest pocket.

"So, are you having a gourmet dog or what?"

 Riley asked, looking up at the menu. Finn had been talking about the arena's legendary foot-long hot dogs ever since he knew he was coming to

the game. Riley's own stomach grumbled as he thought
about the Fully Loaded
Mexi-Dog. Or maybe the
Poutiner-Wiener Platter . . .

"Nah," Finn said. "My dad
says one dog costs almost the
same as last week's groceries."

"Seriously?" said Riley. He hadn't ever
noticed the price.

"I might get some popcorn later," Finn said.

"Sounds good," said Riley. "Just don't get
grease all over our sign."

Riley and Finn followed their dads to their
seats. On the way, Riley grabbed a handful of
napkins from the hot dog cart. Just in case.

★ ★ ★

Halfway through the third period, the hockey
game was tied at 2–2.

"Looks like we might finally get some luck,
eh, Riley?" said Riley's dad. He grabbed Riley's

shoulder and gave it a shake.

"Sure," Riley grunted. His mind had long since skidded away from the ice — pretty much after the first faceoff. The Knights were having a good game, but he and Finn weren't having any luck of their own. The jumbo-screen camera hadn't found them or their bright yellow sign — not even once. Riley knew because he'd been looking up at the screen for nearly the entire game. He had a sore neck to prove it!

"We should dance or something," Finn had suggested a few times. But each time, Riley shot the idea down.

"We need to act like *zombies*," Riley kept saying. "Otherwise our costumes don't make sense."

"But dancing zombies — that's hilarious!"

"It's out of character," Riley insisted.

So whenever the game stopped and music blared,

the boys would stand up and get into their best zombie poses. They tilted their heads to the side and opened their unfocused eyes very wide. Finn went cross-eyed. They let their tongues dangle from their mouths. Finn stuck his arms straight out with limp wrists. Riley held the sign as high as he could over his head and waved it slowly side to side. But the camera didn't seem to care.

Riley watched the minutes on the scoreboard tick away. *Maybe Finn's right. Maybe it's time to try something different*, he thought. But then Riley's eyes landed on the empty super-sized cola in his drink holder. Suddenly he realized he had another problem.

"Dad," Riley whispered. "I have to *go*."

"Now?" Riley's father glanced at the score clock.

"*Now*."

The play on the ice stopped as the opposing team, the Mavericks, called a time out.

"Perfect," said Riley's dad. He stood up and gave Riley's knee a tap. "Let's hustle!"

Riley propped the sign carefully against the seat in front of him. He followed his dad, squeezing past Finn, Finn's dad and the other people in their row, and thinking *hurry, hurry, HURRY!*

A few minutes later, as Riley washed up at the bathroom sink, a thunderous *BOO!* erupted from the crowd. It was so loud it rattled the walls of the men's room.

Riley and his dad dashed out of the bathroom. "What happened?" Riley's dad asked the usher at the entrance to their section.

"Knights took a penalty. The Mavs just went on a power play."

"NO!" said Riley's dad.

They looked up at the jumbo screen. At first a tangle of Mavericks outplayed the Knights near the Knights goalie. But suddenly everything changed. Beau Thomas had the puck! He burst across the rink with no one near him . . . the captain wound up . . . he fired and . . . could it be? YES! *HE SCORED!* A short-handed goal for the Knights!

The buzzer sounded and the crowd went wild. The Knights were up 3–2! A loud dance tune blared from the speakers. Fans were on their feet, cheering and dancing. The fans in the aisle seats high-fived Riley and his dad as they climbed the stairs to their row. Riley could feel the bass notes rumble through his body. His heart felt like it was bouncing on a guitar string.

Then, all of a sudden, the noise from the crowd changed from a victory roar to a giant, ear-splitting laugh. *What happened?* Riley noticed that entire rows of fans had stopped moving. Everyone was staring up at the jumbo screen. Was Sir Pucksley, the Knights mascot, doing something really wild?

Riley turned around to check out the screen for himself.

It wasn't Sir Pucksley.

It was a boy his age — *dressed a lot like Leon Courage!*

There on the jumbo screen was Finn, bobbing and bouncing to the music. He was dancing his heart out. His arms were stretched out from his sides, rippling like overcooked spaghetti noodles. He shook his hips like he was in a hip-hop dance-off. As the music became more frantic, Finn matched his movements to the rhythm. Then he became a dancing robot, moving through poses with mechanical jolting and locking.

The crowd went nuts for Finn. When he shimmied, they laughed. When he popped,

they *woo-hooed*. When
he swayed, they *yeahed*.
Finn had thousands of
eyes locked on him.
But there was *no sign in
sight*!

Riley was fuming as he got to his row.
He squeezed past dancing fans, and finally,
dancing Finn. As Riley shuffled into his seat, he
spotted the sign he'd spent hours designing. It
was on the ground covered in sticky cola and
greasy popcorn bits. Worse, it was folded and
bent more times than a crushed paper airplane.

Riley slammed down into his seat. He was
about to blast Finn about the sign, when the
Knights scored again!

The same feel-good victory song started up.
Sure enough, the jumbo-screen camera zoomed
in on its favourite dancing fan! Finn leaped back
to his feet, jutting his hips left and right, back
and forth. He clutched the back of the seat in
front of him and kicked his legs to either side,
almost doing the splits in the air. The crowd

hooted with delight.

"Have some fun!" said Riley's dad, urging Riley to his feet. He even wiggled Riley's arm to try to jump-start him into a dance. But all Riley could do was stare at Finn. His friend was like a dancing windup doll, fuelled by noise and attention.

#5
insta-fame

"What was it like with all those people watching?" Paulo asked Finn. He and his buddies stopped their hybrid dodge ball/soccer/tag game. It was known as "Paulo-ball," since Paulo brought the ball and made the rules. But that Monday morning before school, even Paulo-ball was taking second place to "Finn Sawchuk, Dance Sensation." That's because Finn's wild jumbo-screen dance from the Knights game had been on the Saturday evening news. The sportscaster had even nicknamed Finn the Knights "Lucky Charm."

"It was *AWWWE*some," said Finn. He made

big gestures in the air with his hands. "Super-loud, too. Right, Riley?"

"Awesome," Riley mumbled. He dug around in his backpack for the movie notebook. He'd heard Finn's story about a dozen times.

"Did you plan that dance?" asked Paulo.

"Not really," said Finn with a shrug. "It was just kind of . . . in the moment."

"But you wore a costume on purpose," said Vijay.

"We were *supposed* to be dressed like zombies," said Riley.

"Zombies? I thought you were Leon Courage."

Riley shot Finn a look that meant *told you!*

"Were you there, too, Riley?" asked Josh. "I didn't see you on TV."

Riley pressed his lips together.

"Guys — someone recorded my dance with their phone and posted it online," Finn said. "It already has, like, five hundred views!"

"Four sixty-three," Riley corrected him. Each time Finn told his story, his video seemed to magically gain a dozen more hits.

"That was *before* school," said Finn. "It's probably way more by now."

"I wonder if it'll go viral?" Vijay said.

Riley gritted his teeth. *Lizard Beast* was supposed to be going viral, not dancing Finn.

"What if you get a thousand views?" asked Josh. "Or a million?"

"You'd be pretty famous," said Paulo.

"Hey, Finn!" A girl's voice sailed through the air toward them. Riley's throat went dry as he spotted Jasmine approaching with Arusha and Claire. He started hunting deeper in his backpack.

"We all saw you on TV," Jasmine gushed.

"Cool," said Finn. He relaxed his knees and

slouched a bit, trying to look casual, as though being on TV happened to him every day.

Jasmine was standing so close that Riley could smell the lemon shampoo she used. His throat tightened even more.

"Was it amazing being on the big screen?" Jasmine asked.

"It was pretty neat, I guess."

What happened to AWWWEsome? Riley wondered.

"Were you nervous?" asked Arusha.

"Not really," Finn replied.

"That song you danced to is the *best*," said Claire. She was giving Finn a big smile. In fact, all the girls were grinning — as if Finn were the genius who'd picked their favourite dance song.

As if Finn were the one who *wrote* the song!

Just then, the bell rang. Riley was glad. He was pretty sure he'd explode if he had to hear Finn's story a thirteenth time.

★ ★ ★

Finn wasn't quite viral online, but he was definitely trending at school. After "O Canada," the principal thanked Finn during announcements for showing his team spirit.

After attendance, Mr. Kim called everyone to the carpet, even though they were supposed to do math at their desks. "Looks like we have a local celebrity in our room," he said. Everyone turned and looked at Finn. A couple of the girls waved their arms around like spaghetti noodles, just like Finn had when he'd danced.

"I thought we'd all enjoy seeing the news clip. Is that okay with you, Finn?"

Riley, sitting beside Finn, noticed his friend's face was calm as he nodded. But from the shoulders down, Finn's body was squirming with excited energy.

Mr. Kim told Arusha to turn down the lights as he powered

up the whiteboard. He navigated to Finn's video on the news channel's website and pressed play.

The music started to thump through the speakers and Finn's dancing image appeared. The sportscaster narrated the story:

A young fan dances to the beat at Saturday afternoon's Knights game. His moves inspire the crowd. Even our Knights, who've been unlucky in their last few match-ups, were charmed into scoring again. Could this young man be our team's new lucky charm?

On screen, Finn was shaking and shimmying like a hip-hop octopus. He bounced and hula-danced as the sportscaster talked about the arena's "electric atmosphere."

When the video ended, the whole class applauded. Jasmine, Arusha and Claire leaped to their feet and started dancing. They pulled Finn to his feet to join them. Finn's freckled face was as red as a ripe tomato.

But he stood between the girls
and did his famous dance.

The more the class clapped
and cheered, the more Finn loos-
ened his moves. He danced more
wildly. His body looked like it was
made of rippling rubber. Students
pumped their hands in the air and
chanted, "GO Fi-INN! . . . *GO! GO!
. . . Go Fi-INN! . . . GO! GO!* . . ."

Riley watched as others
joined the dance. Even Vijay and
Josh got into it. "You, too, Mr. Kim!" someone
shouted. But Mr. Kim just smiled and said that
dancing was best left to the experts.

"Can we watch it again?" asked Paulo. Riley
knew that Paulo was probably just trying to get
out of the math. But several girls (including
Jasmine!) began to *beg* Mr. Kim to *please, please,
please* play it again.

"Maybe after lunch," said Mr. Kim. "For
now, let's get back to our desks. We have a
busy day." The teacher gave Finn a thumbs-up.

"That looked like fun," he said. "Way to go!"

As they got up from the carpet, some of the girls sang the song Finn had danced to. Josh asked Finn to sign his shoe. Ella asked him to sign her arm with a marker. (Riley noticed he did it, too, when Mr. Kim wasn't watching.) Riley saw Jasmine smile at Finn across the room.

Riley couldn't wait to get going on that math!

Scene: "THE BIG PLAN"

Riley as Rocket

Finn as Flapjack

Slow-Mo as Lizard Beast (voice by Riley)

Lizard Beast and Rocket look at a map lying on the ground.

ROCKET: I believe the zombies will strike here first, Lizard Beast.

Rocket moves his arm to point to a spot on the map.

LIZARD BEAST: We must warn Flapjack. our faithful ally.

ROCKET: I agree. Where is he?

Flapjack runs into view.

~~FLAPJACK: The zombies are coming. We have to go!~~

FLAPJACK: PHOTOBOMB!

Note: **Messed up by Finn's photobomb gag with Flapjack. Now a deleted scene**

#6
Finn's Big Break

"My mom and dad are taking us to a resort in Mexico next Christmas," said Riley. He was nestled in an old brown beanbag chair with his movie notebook. Riley and Finn were at Finn's apartment after school. They needed the time to work on *Lizard Beast*.

"That's cool," said Finn. His voice sounded a million miles away. He was staring at the screen on his dad's old computer. Balanced on his lap was the mini keyboard he'd borrowed from Riley. Finn tapped out a jerky tune using the stardust sound.

"Actually, it gave me an idea for our movie," Riley continued in a louder voice. "Remember how we were trying to come up with a reason that zombies appear on Lizard Beast's island?"

"Mmm," said Finn.

"Well, what if there was a resort on the other side of the island, where people go on vacation? Maybe some weird chemical got into the drinking water, and it turns the tourists into zombies."

"Sure," Finn said, his voice still sounding far away. He put the keyboard on the floor as he clicked something on the screen with his mouse. "I've never been to a resort."

"You could imagine it, though — right?"

"I guess," murmured Finn. "Why would they build a resort on an island with lizard monsters?"

Riley bit his lip. It was a good point. "It's a big island. Maybe they just didn't know."

"Couldn't they see Lizard Beast's lair from

the plane — *HA! NO WAY!*" Finn shouted, suddenly alert. He spun around in his swivel chair with a huge grin on his face.

"What?" Riley asked. He dropped his notebook, jumped from the beanbag and joined Finn at the computer.

"Look! *Seven hundred and sixteen views,*" Finn said triumphantly.

Riley looked at the view counter underneath the *Knights Lucky Charm Dance* video that had been posted online. "Were you looking at this the whole time?" Riley asked. No wonder Finn was talking as if his brain were in outer space!

A blast of cold air filled the room as the door to the apartment patio slid open. Finn's dad, wearing his old unzipped Knights parka, stepped inside. His phone was pressed against his ear. "Sure, I'll tell him," he said into the phone.

"Dad — *seven hundred and sixteen views*!" Finn whispered, gesturing to the computer.

Mr. Sawchuk gave Finn

a thumbs up. "So, Finn," he said as he pushed the button to end the call, "what would you say to an interview with Buster and Jax tomorrow morning?"

Finn's green eyes bulged like basketballs. "What?!" he shouted.

What?! Riley thought. Buster and Jax were the hosts of *The Knight Shift*, the city's most popular hockey TV talk show. They sometimes did serious interviews with the Knights. But they were most famous for their fun stuff, like pulling pranks on the players in the locker room. Riley's dad never missed an episode.

"Your uncle Claude bumped into Jax at the station," Finn's dad explained. "He mentioned that the lucky dance kid on the news was his nephew. Next thing you know, Jax says he wants to have you on the show!"

"On TV?" Finn asked. Riley pictured the entire school lining up in front of Finn for him to sign their shoes, their backpacks, their T-shirts, their arms . . . maybe even their foreheads!

"No. It's for their podcast. You'll call them

tomorrow morning, and they'll do the interview over the phone."

"Cool!" said Finn.

"Right on. I'm going to go call Grandma to let her know." Mr. Sawchuk went back out onto the patio.

Finn twirled in his chair. "I wonder what they'll ask me?" Finn asked. He pushed off the floor to get more momentum. He was whipping around so fast it made Riley dizzy just watching.

"Hopefully nothing about hockey," Riley said. He knew way more about the Knights than Finn. Finn didn't know any stats — he even got the players' names and numbers mixed up sometimes. But of course, the interview wouldn't be about any of that. It would be all about Finn's moment of jumbo-screen fame.

"Stop spinning!" Riley said, filled with a sudden inspiration. He grabbed the armrests to steady Finn's chair. "When Buster and Jax ask you about your dance, make sure you tell them *why* you were dressed up!"

Finn stumbled off the seat and collapsed onto the floor. "Whoa . . . oh boy! I think . . . I'm gonna be . . . Nope — he's okay, folks!" Finn shook his head and sat up straight.

"Finn, listen to me. Tell Buster and Jax that we had costumes on to promote our movie. You can tell them about the blog and the movie festival . . ." Riley was suddenly pumped. He knew that thousands of people tuned into Buster and Jax's TV show. Their fans must listen to their podcast, too. He and Finn still had a chance to tell the world about *Lizard Beast versus the Zombie Horde*!

"What if they don't ask me the right questions?" Finn asked.

"Just find a way to work it in." Riley reached for the movie notebook. "In fact, let's write a little script for your interview. No, not a script — what do they call that movie thing? That line the guy with the deep movie voice says during a movie trailer, to make it sound exciting?"

Finn shrugged.

"That's it — *a tagline*!" Riley said, answering his own question. He remembered the term from animation camp. "You can tell them about our movie with an action-packed tagline. I'll work on it right now."

Riley nestled back into the beanbag chair and bent his head over the notebook. Meanwhile, Finn was back in the swivel chair spinning in circles.

TAGline Ideas

Lizard Beast is alone against the zombies until he meets Special Ops soldiers Rocket and Flapjack. But can a lizard ever trust human beings? (Too long)

One Lizard. Two Men. Lots of Zombies. Get ready for ACTION! (meh . . .)

One Lizard. Two Guys. Tons of zombies. What could go wrong? (NOT BAD . . .)

★ ★ ★

That night Riley was jumping around playing air guitar. He was cranking out the rock and roll theme to Buster and Jax's show. He could barely wait to hear Finn give a shout-out for their movie on the podcast. Everyone at school would be talking about it. Mr. Kim would probably play it for the class. Riley pictured himself signing Jasmine's arm . . .

As he leaped around his bedroom, Riley spotted the purple clip-on bow tie he'd worn to his cousin's wedding. He stopped dancing, grabbed it from the dresser and clipped it to the collar of his pyjamas. He checked himself out in the mirror. A scene began to play in his imagination . . .

Movie-maker Riley Foster, dressed in a swanky purple tuxedo with matching bow tie, climbs up onto a brightly lit stage. A large crowd gazes back at him. Everyone is dressed in fancy suits and sparkly dresses.

RILEY: I'd like to thank everyone here tonight. Winning the Best Picture Award means a lot to me . . .

Wait a minute!

Riley raced from his bedroom and down the hall to the bathroom. He grabbed Kennedy's special, *don't-you-dare-use-this-Riley*, celebrity-brand shampoo for long curly hair from the bathtub ledge. It was a slim, silver-coloured bottle. It was topped with a shiny plastic cap that looked like a large diamond. It always made Riley think of a fancy trophy. He ran back to his room, repositioned himself in front of his mirror and resumed his scene.

Riley accepts his Best Picture Award from a lady in a long, shimmering gown.

RILEY: This means so much to me. (He clutches the silver award to his chest). Thank you to my family and friends, and especially to you, Slow-Mo. Without you, there would be no Lizard Beast.

And to my girlfriend, Jasmine Santos — thank you for your support. By the way, congratulations for winning Best Actress tonight, Jasmine . . .

Riley heard a shuffling sound near his bedroom door. He jumped and lost his grip on the bottle. The cap flew off as the bottle hit the floor. He spun around to see Kennedy, dressed in her fluffy pink robe, standing in the doorway.

"Nice tie," Kennedy began to tease, then stopped. Her gaze, like Riley's, was pulled to the floor. They both watched in horror as her precious shampoo glugged out of the silver bottle and soaked into Riley's bedroom rug. Riley fell to his knees. He tried to scoop the liquid back into the bottle, but it was useless.

"Stop doing that!" Kennedy shouted, her eyes wide. "You're getting carpet fuzz in it! *And what are you doing with my stuff?! DAA-AAD!*"

#7
Finn
Fever

"Ready?" said Riley's dad from the front seat of the car. His cell phone was hooked into the stereo. He'd downloaded Finn's podcast so they could all listen to it on the ride to school.

"Sure," Kennedy mumbled from the back seat, texting her friends. Her body was scrunched against the door as far away from Riley as she could get. She was showing him exactly how she felt about last night's shampoo incident. But Riley wasn't thinking about Kennedy.

"Turn it up!" Riley said, leaning forward. He didn't want to miss Finn's delivery of the awesome tagline he'd finally settled on: Lizard

Beast has met his match: a horde of mutant zombies with only one thing on their brains — LIZARD BRAINS!

The podcast began:

BUSTER: Mornin'. Knights Fans! You're with Buster and Jax for your favourite segment of the day. *Fan Fever*. We've got Finn on the line. You may know him as the young dancing sensation from last Saturday's home game. Should we be calling you "Finn, The Lucky Charm"?

JAX: Or maybe "Finn Courage"? We saw that funky outfit you had on . . .

BUSTER: Whoa-ho!

JAX: Don't knock it. man. The ladies love that Leon guy. right Finn?

(Buster and Jax chuckle)

BUSTER: So. tell us. Finn — are you a

big Knights fan?

FINN: Oh. yeah. You bet!

JAX: Do you play hockey?

FINN: Sure! Well. floor hockey. In gym.

BUSTER: Floor hockey — man! Those were the days. eh. Jax?

JAX: I was a BEAST on the gym floor. that's for sure. Unstoppable!

Beast! thought Riley. *Jax just said "beast"! Come on, Finn — it's perfect. Say something about LIZARD BEAST . . . right now!*

BUSTER: Unstoppable — ha! That's because you didn't have to skate. I'm telling you. Finn. when Jax laces up and hits the ice. he looks more like he's doing your dance than playing hockey.

(Chuckle. chuckle. chuckle)

Riley felt his fists clench. *Were they just going to make dumb jokes the whole time? When was Finn going to mention their movie?*

"Turn it up some more, Dad," said Riley, as if the louder the podcast, the sooner he'd hear what he wanted to.

JAX: So tell us. Finn. What inspired your dance?

YES! Here we go, thought Riley, relieved. *Finn had to mention the movie now. It was perfect . . .*

FINN: Um . . . the music. I guess?

NOOOOOOO! Not the music — our movie!

FINN: And. uh . . .

LIZARD BEAST VERSUS THE

ZOMBIE HORDE!

FINN: Well . . . the game. It was an awesome game. I'd never been to a game before.

BUSTER: Whoa-ho! We've got a Knights game newbie, Jax. We might have to do something about that.

JAX: I'll have to check the vault for tickets after this segment. (Chuckle, chuckle, chuckle.) What do you think, Finn? The Knights need their Lucky Charm at their next home game, right?

FINN: That would be awesome!

BUSTER: With those dance moves, Finn — you're the king of awesomeness!

This time, Riley could hear Finn joining in on the cheesy radio chuckle-fest.

JAX: All right, Finn. Thanks for being such a great sport and coming on the show. And Knights fans — be

sure to check out Finn's lucky
dance video on our web page.

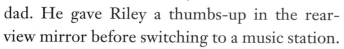

And that was it for Buster
and Jax and Finn.

Finn had said only a few
words. And none of them were
about Lizard Beast or zombies
or class blogs or movie festivals or
Riley Foster.

"Tell Finn we heard him.
He's famous!" said Riley's
dad. He gave Riley a thumbs-up in the rear-
view mirror before switching to a music station.

Riley slumped back in the seat, dreams of
going viral *crushed*.

"Riley!" Finn dashed toward the classroom coat
hooks, where Riley was hanging up his parka.
"Guess what I got?"

"Your own private podcast?" Riley snapped.

"No," said Finn. He stopped in his tracks. "What's that supposed to mean?"

"Oh, come on, 'king of awesomeness.' You know what I mean."

"Not really. So, you heard the podcast?" Finn's face was eager.

"Of course I did," said Riley. "*All* of it."

"Pretty funny, right? Did you hear when Buster made fun of Jax?"

"Hilarious," said Riley, his voice dry. "What's wrong?"

"Why didn't you say our tagline?" Riley demanded.

Finn blinked. "They didn't ask me about that stuff."

"Of course they didn't. How would they know? You were supposed to bring it up yourself at the right time — remember?"

"But there wasn't a right time," Finn insisted.

"There were *lots* of right times. At least two or three."

"But the interview was super short, and —"

"*SO WAS THE TAGLINE!*" Riley growled.

Finn sucked in his breath. "Sorry for not mentioning *your* movie during *my* interview."

"It's *our* movie!"

"Yeah, right."

"It was the perfect chance to get us an online audience for the festival. I can't believe you blew it."

Finn bit his bottom lip so hard Riley could see it turn bright white. But Riley didn't care. He was mad, too. Didn't Finn realize this was probably their last chance to make *Lizard Beast* famous?

"Sorry for not blasting *your* name all over the airwaves," Finn said before stomping away.

Clueless! Riley thought.

When Mr. Kim announced they'd have time to

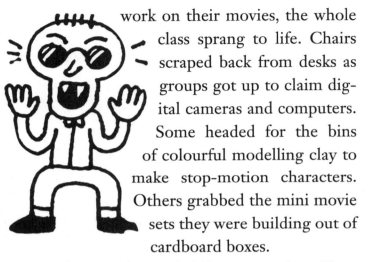

work on their movies, the whole class sprang to life. Chairs scraped back from desks as groups got up to claim digital cameras and computers. Some headed for the bins of colourful modelling clay to make stop-motion characters. Others grabbed the mini movie sets they were building out of cardboard boxes.

"I'll get a laptop," Riley grunted at Finn. These were the first words he'd said since their blow-up by the coat hooks. They didn't have a choice now — it was movie time, and they had to talk to each other.

When Riley returned to the table where they usually worked, he found Finn. And Jasmine, Arusha and Claire. The girls crowded around Finn in a tight semicircle.

"What are you guys doing?" Riley asked. Then he noticed that Finn was playing his mini keyboard.

"He's playing us a Leon Courage song," said Jasmine, her eyes twinkling.

"'Luv U Thru Time'?" asked Riley, rolling his eyes toward the ceiling.

"Hardly," said Claire with a snort. "It's 'Just As U R.'"

"Oh," said Riley, sliding into his chair. "All his songs sound the same."

The three girls glared at Riley. Clearly this had not been the right thing to say. Riley cleared his throat and opened up his movie notebook. He was careful to place his arm to shield his notes from "the competition."

"Hey, Finn," said Riley. "I was thinking that we should try to finish scene five for the sneak preview."

But Finn didn't reply. He just squeezed his eyes shut and pounded on the notes. He was acting like some sort of musical genius. He seemed so deep in concentration he couldn't hear the outside world. Riley

noticed that Jasmine was swaying to the music and tapping her hand against her leg.

"We really need to add some music to our movie," Jasmine said.

"It has to be sad, though," said Claire.

"Of course," said Jasmine. "Did you listen to any of the music on the computer that Mr. Kim said we could use?"

Arusha scrunched up her nose. "It's kind of . . . *blah*," she said.

Then it will be perfect for your boring movie! Riley thought. He knew that Jasmine's group was making a movie about a teenage girl who falls in love with a half-Pegasus, half-human dude named Alfonzo. He and Finn laughed about it all the time. Riley smirked and poked Finn in the leg, trying to share a laugh. But Finn kept his focus on the keyboard.

"I'll be over there," Riley grumbled to Finn. Clutching his notebook, Riley headed for a free table in the corner and sat down to work alone.

*Lizard Beast versus the Zombie Horde needs **MORE ACTION** — or a **REALLY BIG TWIST.***

Some ideas:

* Flapjack's brain gets EATEN by zombies (too gross for class blog)
* Flapjack gets CAPTURED by zombies (meh)
* Flapjack IS a zombie (hmmm . . . that could work!)

#8
Finn the Virus

"So why aren't you the one going with Finn?" Vijay asked. Riley was waiting outside school for his mom's SUV. Vijay and Paulo, also waiting for rides, were messing around with Paulo's dodge ball.

"Where?" Riley asked.

"To the Knights game tomorrow night," said Paulo.

"The Knights game?" Riley repeated.

"Finn got free tickets from Buster and Jax. Didn't you know? He's been bragging about it nonstop all day," Paulo said. He slammed the ball against the brick wall of the school.

"You mean, he didn't ask you first?" Vijay said. He caught the bouncing ball and stared at Riley. "I thought you guys were best friends."

"Oh, yeah. He asked me," said Riley, not sure why he was lying. "I'm busy, though."

"Bummer," said Vijay.

"Finn should have asked *me*," said Paulo. He tore the ball out of Vijay's hands and began to dribble it. He wove it through his legs like a pro basketball player. "He knows I'm a Knights freak."

"Or me," said Vijay. "I could show off my own sweet moves on the jumbo screen." Vijay twisted his lower body, like he was twirling an invisible hula hoop.

"Guess you're not as pretty as *Jasmine*, Vijay," said Paulo, fluttering his eyelids.

Riley's eyebrows nearly reached the sky.

"*WHAT?!?*"

"He asked *Jasmine*.

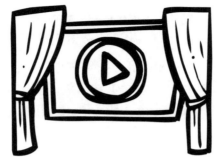

Can you believe it?" Vijay laughed. "And she said yes. So I guess it's a date."

"Finn's dad's going, too," said Paulo.

"I know, but still . . ."

Riley couldn't believe it. He'd treated Finn to his first-ever Knights game — *the game that had apparently changed his life*! And Finn hadn't even bothered to invite him back. Not only that, he'd gone behind Riley's back and asked the one girl he knew Riley kind of, sort of liked.

"Maybe he'll rent a limo now that he's such a big superstar," Vijay said. "And bring roses for Jasmine, of course."

"I still say he should have asked me," said Paulo. He bounced the ball so hard it almost landed on the school roof.

★ ★ ★

The next day during first period, Riley sniffed the air.

What was that smell?

Riley looked up from his math sheet and sniffed again. A strong, sweet scent was wafting off Finn's neck.

"Ew. Are you wearing . . . *perfume*?" Riley whispered.

"No," Finn whispered back sharply. He erased on his paper so hard he tore a hole in it.

"Well, I smell something gross," Riley insisted a little more loudly. Maybe a bit of embarrassment would be good for Finn. Maybe he'd stop acting like a spoiled celebrity.

"It's body spray, okay!" Finn hissed back. He twisted himself as far as he could from Riley.

A loud "Ha!" escaped from Riley, and Mr. Kim looked in their direction. Riley coughed to cover up and went back to his work. But inside, he was thinking: *Body spray? On* that *body? What a dork!*

Later, when the class got bonus movie time, Finn didn't even try to join Riley at their usual table. Finn was an expert at getting out of work during class. He was always getting up for a sip of water, or to sharpen a pencil crayon, or to float from group to group to borrow an eraser. But this was the first time Finn had used his talent to avoid working with Riley on *Lizard Beast*.

Riley tried to shrug it off and work on his own. But soon he broke down. The sneak preview was less than a week away! He and Finn needed to finish a blockbuster, Best Picture–worthy scene to showcase. So when he spotted Finn settling in with Jasmine and her group, he decided he had to do something.

He marched across the room. "Hey, Leon,"

Riley said sarcastically. "Time to work on our movie."

"He's making some original music for us," said Claire.

"But he's not in your group!"

"Mr. Kim said we could work with other groups, remember?"

Arusha said. Turning to Finn, she added, "Don't worry. We'll put your name in our credits."

"Thanks," said Finn. He fluttered his fingers on the keyboard with drama. Riley noticed that Jasmine had a big, bright smile on her face.

Way to help the competition, Finn! Riley thought. Out loud, he said, "Um — you guys know that's actually *my* keyboard, right?"

"Oh," said Jasmine. "Does that mean Finn can't help us?" The light went out of her face like a blown-out birthday candle.

"What? No . . . I just . . ." Riley said, feeling flustered. "Never mind. Whatever. Finn — I'm over there when you're ready to *work*." Riley spoke the last word sharply before stomping away, but not before hearing Jasmine tell Finn that he had to make the music sound "really, really sad and tragic."

Sad and tragic, sad and tragic, Riley grumbled to himself. *Finn Sawchuk is sad and tragic! He just* wants to get close enough to *Jasmine* so she smells his disgusting perfume and starts dreaming about their "big date"!

Suddenly, Riley had the perfect idea for a bit of revenge. He tore a piece of paper from the back of his movie notebook and wrote a note. He disguised his printing by making it bigger and neater than usual, and he didn't sign it:

FINN IS WEARING LOTS OF PERFUME. SOME PEOPLE ARE GETTING HEADACHES.

Riley snuck a look toward Mr. Kim's desk to make sure no one was around. While pretending to put a piece of paper in the recycling bin, he slipped the note onto the teacher's desk.

Not much later, Riley saw Mr. Kim go to his desk and read the note. The teacher called Finn up to see him. Riley doodled in his notebook, pretending not to notice. Meanwhile, he was thinking, *Sniff test — you're busted!*

Mr. Kim said something very quietly to Finn. He was probably reminding him of the signs on the school's front door: *NO NUTS. NO FISH. NO SCENTED PRODUCTS.*

Finn said something in reply to Mr. Kim. He left the classroom and returned a few minutes later. His face was shiny and red, and his sleeves were pushed up past his elbows. It looked as though he'd scrubbed up in the bathroom. Even the hair on his forehead was wet.

As he made his way back toward Jasmine and her group, red-faced Finn shot Riley a glare full of raging fire.

Finn must have known that Riley had ratted him out.

And Riley looked right back at Finn with a triumphant smirk.

Big Twist

FLAPJACK IS THE ONE "CREATING" THE ZOMBIES (YES!!)

BUT HOW?

* With mind control? (boring)
* With a zombie-making machine? (meh)
* With a disgusting virus potion that totally REEKS? (PERFECT!!)

#9
Rise of the Mutant Ponies

"Riley — the game's about to start!" Riley heard his dad call to him. He was in the basement storage room almost buried in a stack of cardboard boxes.

"I'm looking for movie props," Riley shouted back.

"Okay. But I made popcorn . . ."

Riley's stomach growled and his mouth began to water. He loved popcorn, especially the way his dad made it, with extra butter and salt. "Later!" Riley called back. He heard his dad settling in to watch the game. A big section of the Fosters' basement was set up like a movie theatre. There was a huge TV screen on the wall and a special reclining couch. Riley heard the seat squeak as his dad let out a satisfied, "*Ahhhhhh!*"

As much as Riley craved a mouthful of crunchy, buttery popcorn, he did not want to watch the Knights game. Finn and Jasmine were lurking somewhere in that crowd, waiting for their turn on the jumbo screen. What if the camera zoomed in on them? What if Riley was forced to watch their dancing and good times on the big screen in his very own basement?

So Riley focused on creating a blowout movie scene for the sneak preview. He was going through boxes of old junk, hoping to find something. Somewhere there had to be a one of a kind prop that would add a wow factor to *Lizard Beast versus the Zombie Horde*. He liked his Big New Twist — that Flapjack was the bad guy creating the zombies. Still, he needed a way to show just how twisted Flapjack really was.

Riley plunged his hands into one box after another. He was on the hunt, though not really sure what he was looking for. So far, he'd found a baby mobile with fuzzy teddy bears, toddler-sized swimming flippers, mismatched puzzle pieces and a box of old crafting supplies. But nothing *wow*.

Riley was about to give up when he spotted a small box at the very back of the bottom shelf. He had to flatten his body onto the floor and reach his arms as far as they could go to touch it. He batted at the box until he could edge it forward.

He sat up, spitting out a mouthful of dust. Inside the box was Kennedy's ancient collection of plastic winged horses.

"The Magic Rainbow Riders," Riley whispered to himself with a shudder. "Ick." He was instantly haunted by memories of Kennedy making Riley play Magic Rainbow Riders with her. Kennedy had forced him to braid, brush and tie girly bows in the horses' manes and tails. Then, they would send the Riders on dumb adventures where the boy horses rescued the girl horses. Or sometimes the girls rescued the boys. Whatever happened, Kennedy always made the horses smooch and get married.

Gross! Riley thought. *We should have had epic horse battles. Not that these guys look like combat warriors.*

Unless . . .

Riley looked at the open box of craft supplies beside him, then back at the Magic Rainbow Riders. An idea began to form in his movie-making mind. He found a black marker and tested it on the craft box to make sure it still had juice. He picked up a light-blue pony and gave it a pair of evil eyebrows.

Not bad.

He drew on a moustache and a pointy beard.

Even better.

Next, Riley picked up a lilac-coloured pony.

He gave this one crazy eyes, with each of its black pupils aimed in a different direction. He drew an open mouth and two rows of jagged teeth, like the jaws of a great white shark.

Riley was getting excited. These mutant horse creatures would look *amazing* next to Slow-Mo on video. He picked up a peach-coloured horse and gave it a stubbly chin, an eye patch and a skull-and-crossbones tattoo on its back. He ripped off one of its plastic wings to make it look more like a fighter. He found a pair of scissors in the craft box and began to hack at the horse's mane. Why not give them all edgy haircuts! One by one, their tails got sliced into ragged shreds of pastel purple, yellow and blue. Riley chopped their manes into short, spiky dos. (He left one of the Riders alone — a pink one. He could film it in the process of being zombified!)

Riley spread the gang of mutant ponies in front of him. *THESE are enemy creatures worthy of mighty Lizard Beast*, he thought. He was pretty sure he'd found his wow factor.

NEW SCENE: "The Zombie Virus Test"

Flapjack is alone in his tent mixing up the stinking zombie virus potion. He pours some into the bucket his pet pink horse is drinking from.

In stop-motion. the pink pony goes from looking cute. to having evil eyes. to growing a nasty. pointy beard. to gaining ripped muscles . . . and finally . . . sprouting jagged teeth.

The mutant pony gallops around the tent. She snarls like a hungry zombie. Flapjack laughs like a maniac.

#10
finn-heads

"Where is everyone?" Riley asked Paulo. Paulo was alone, kicking the dodge ball against the school wall.

"Over there," Paulo said. He pointed toward the schoolyard and gave the ball another hard kick.

Riley followed Paulo's finger. In the distance, Finn sat on top of the monkey bars. He was swinging one of his legs back and forth and waving his hands in the air. Jasmine was on the platform below, making similar gestures. A group of kids from their class was hanging around below, eyes glued to them.

Riley drifted over to see what was going on. When he reached the play structure, he moved away as far as he could be and still see and hear the action. He pulled his movie notebook from his backpack and pretended to read.

"We were on the jumbo screen *twice*," Riley heard Jasmine brag. He noticed that her jacket was unzipped, showing off a bright orange T-shirt. The words *BUSTER AND JAX: THE KNIGHT SHIFT!* were splattered across the front in spiky blue letters.

"Once we were on with Sir Pucksley," Finn said.

"He did the lucky dance with us," said Jasmine.

"Remember when he tried to mess up my hair?" said Finn. He and Jasmine laughed as they passed their story back and forth. It was like they were two power forwards on an offensive rush.

"I watched the whole game on TV," said Navdeep from the crowd. "I didn't see you guys. Not even once."

"Not everything from the jumbo screen gets on TV," said Finn. He hooked his knees around the monkey bars and hung upside down.

"Were you on the news again?" someone asked.

"Why would they be?" said Vijay. "The Knights didn't even score. Some lucky charm, Finn!"

"Did you post any videos online?" someone else asked.

"No," said Jasmine. Riley thought she sounded a bit annoyed with her audience.

"We didn't take a video," said upside-down Finn, his face a deep red from the blood rushing to his scalp. He grabbed the bars and flipped down onto the snowy gravel below.

"Is your old video going viral yet?" another kid asked.

"It has two thousand and four views," said Finn in a louder-than-usual voice.

Mostly from you clicking on it a thousand times! thought Riley.

"But that's what it had two days ago," someone else pointed out.

Exactly, thought Riley. *Hardly viral.*

"You should have at least taken some selfies to show us," said Ella.

"We were *dancing*!" Jasmine said, clearly frustrated. "Just because you didn't see it doesn't mean it wasn't awesome." She jumped down from the platform and started to walk away.

"Hey — did the Kiss Patrol find you?" asked Vijay, elbowing Navdeep in the side. The two boys laughed. At every Knights game, the Kiss Patrol Camera zoomed in on couples in the crowd — even old people — and put them on screen. It wouldn't turn away until they kissed. (There was always a prize for best smooch.) Vijay puckered up and kissed the air as everyone laughed.

Jasmine spun around. "You guys are gross!" she said. She turned and left in a huff.

The bell rang. Riley kept his distance from the group bounding toward the school. But he noticed how Finn's shoulders were hunched up to his ears. Jokes were still being launched at him about his "date" with Jasmine.

Finally, Finn stopped and loudly announced, "Keep it up and I won't take *any of you* to the next game!"

The jokers quit laughing.

"Seriously? You got some more tickets?" asked Navdeep.

Finn shrugged his shoulders. "Maybe." He stuffed his hands in his jacket pockets and strode ahead of the group. His head was now held high.

Riley knew Finn was bluffing. Why would Buster and Jax keep giving him prizes? The Knights hadn't even won!

"Take me?" Vijay called as he raced to catch up with Finn.

★ ★ ★

Rumours of hockey tickets, Knights freebies and more swirled around Riley's classroom all morning.

Did you hear? Finn's getting more tickets from Buster and Jax . . .

Well I heard he's going to try and take the whole class. The Knights need extra luck to start winning again . . .

Oh yeah? I heard he's going to get us a warm-up skate with the Knights before the game . . .

And he's even going to get us VIP passes for Leon Courage next time he comes to town!

Riley stayed out of it. But it was impossible to ignore the fact that all his friends were turning into zombified Finn-Heads! Whenever someone asked Finn if he could keep his promises, he would flash the piece of paper he kept in his pocket. (He claimed it was the private number he'd used to call Buster and Jax's podcast.) And just like that, Finn zombified even more followers.

But being a Finn-Head wasn't all fun and games.

"You two look like twins," Navdeep told Finn when he removed his sweatshirt. Underneath, Finn was wearing the exact same orange Knight Shift shirt that Jasmine had on. "Or maybe — boyfriend/girl-friend?" Navdeep added with a laugh.

Jasmine, who was nearby, was furious. "You said you weren't going to wear yours today," she scolded Finn. "You promised!"

Riley watched as Jasmine stormed from the classroom. She grabbed her gym bag on the way out. *She's probably going to change into her gym shirt to un-twin herself from Finn*, Riley thought.

Riley noticed Finn's face fall as he watched Jasmine stomp away. But he quickly turned to Navdeep with a kingly look. "Guess you don't like free hockey games," Finn said coldly.

"I was just . . ." Navdeep tried.

Finn turned his back on Navdeep. He was

sending a clear message to everyone: *If you cross King Finn, you're out of luck!*

NEW SCENE: "The Making of the Zombie Horde"

Riley as Flapjack, Rocket, Lizard Beast and Random Voices

Setting: Tent on the tropical beach. Flapjack's voice can be heard inside.

FLAPJACK: Drink up, my friends. Great powers await you! DON'T TRY TO RESIST!

Rocket and Lizard Beast arrive outside the tent's door.

ROCKET: Flapjack, are you okay? What is that awful smell?

FLAPJACK (from inside tent): I'm fine. Just finishing my dinner!

LIZARD BEAST: Are you eating rotten fish with cheap

---

perfume sauce? It STINKS!

ROCKET: We're looking for the rest of the team. Are they in there with you?

FLAPJACK (from inside tent): No. It's just me. I'm totally alone. All by myself.

Rocket and Lizard Beast walk away. But zombie grunts and shuffling zombie footsteps can be heard inside the tent.

FLAPJACK (from inside tent): Mwa-ha-ha-ha-ha-ha!

#11
(very) special effects

"If you're finished with Science, you can work on your movies," said Mr. Kim. "Remember — sneak preview in two days."

Riley whipped through the last bit of the write-up for his experiment and headed straight for the laptops. Two days left — *as if he needed reminding*! Riley had been worrying nonstop about how to turn his scattered bits of video footage into an epic, Best Picture–worthy movie scene. (He'd managed to squash down his other big worry. He didn't know what Mr. Kim would do when he found out that Riley was working on his film alone.)

Riley took his bright orange flash drive from his pocket and popped it into one of the laptops. He opened up a video that showed mutant horses galloping in an empty frame. It looked like they were floating in black space. Riley had shot it against a homemade "green screen." Then he had used his editing program to cut out the electric green background from behind the running horses. What he needed was a video of Slow-Mo he'd already shot. Then he could layer the horses right onto the Slow-Mo video, so that it looked like one complete scene.

As Riley navigated through old video clips on his drive, he noticed that the air smelled sweet. Kind of like lemon meringue pie.

"Are those old Magic Rainbow Riders?" said a voice beside Riley.

Sure enough, Jasmine (and her lemony-fresh hair) had slipped behind the laptop next to Riley's.

Riley cleared his throat. "These? Uh . . . yeah." He quickly added, "They're my sister's old toys. They're not mine or anything."

"They look *totally* creepy," Jasmine said with admiration.

"Really?" Riley looked back at his screen. When he looked at the horses, all he saw was the rush job he'd done cutting around them. Stray green pixels clung to the horses' edges, especially their tails. To Riley, the horses looked more sloppy than creepy. But if Jasmine said so, maybe they weren't so bad.

"I like their tattoos," Jasmine said. She turned to her own laptop and opened her movie file.

Riley felt his cheeks grow warm. It was hard to concentrate with Jasmine beside him. He wanted to say something — *anything* — to keep the conversation going.

"How's your . . . *uh* . . . project coming along?" He heard himself stumble over his words.

"Fine," said Jasmine. She leaned so close to her screen that her nose almost touched it. She seemed deeply focused on an editing task, something that Riley could relate to. He knew he shouldn't interrupt, but . . .

"So, is Finn still helping you with your soundtrack?"

Jasmine whipped around to face Riley. "Why is everyone still asking me about Finn? It wasn't a date, okay? *Yeesh!*"

"No! I didn't mean that," Riley protested. "It's just that Finn basically bailed on our movie. I wondered what he's been doing all this time."

"Oh. Sorry." Jasmine turned back to her screen. "Finn made some music for us last week. But I don't know what he's working on now."

Riley and Jasmine both glanced across the classroom. Finn was sitting alone with Riley's keyboard, wearing headphones. His shoulders bounced and shook as he played music no one else could hear.

"He's probably working on a dumb song to get those podcast guys' attention," said Jasmine, rolling her eyes. "He should give it up. No one thinks he's the Lucky Charm anymore."

"No kidding," Riley said. He'd noticed that the freebies-from-Finn rumours had almost died out. There were fewer Finn-Heads hanging around their "king," now that it was clear Finn didn't really have the power to keep his promises.

Jasmine shook her head. "I'll bet he wears that shirt every day this week." She was eyeing his bright orange shirt, the one that had made her Finn's twin. Riley could actually see a bit of orange peeking out of the top of Jasmine's hoodie (which was zipped up all the way and tied tight at the top). "Did you ever notice how Finn wears the same clothes again and again . . . a lot?" Jasmine asked.

Riley did notice. He knew it was because Finn and his dad didn't have a washing machine in their apartment. (And sometimes Mr. Sawchuk forgot to go to the laundromat.) But he laughed with Jasmine like it was a big joke. "Yeah," he said. "He'll have to start putting on more of that fancy *perfume* if he wears it one more time."

Jasmine giggled. "You smelled that, too?" she said. "He wore some to the hockey game. It's like he took a bath in it."

"Ew," said Riley.

As they laughed, Jasmine glanced again at the videos on Riley's laptop. "Hey, how did you cut the horses out like that?" She leaned over and turned Riley's laptop toward herself.

"I did it at home. With a green screen and editing software," said Riley.

"That's really neat," said Jasmine. She looked interested. Even impressed!

Riley inched his chair a bit closer. "The horse video has an alpha channel. That means the black stuff behind them is really invisible space. So when I put the horses on top of another video like this one" — he pointed to the Slow-Mo video — "they'll just blend right in, like they're part of this scene."

Jasmine nodded, then added, "*Awwwww!*

He's so cute!" as Riley played a clip of Slow-Mo walking across his living room floor. Some people freaked out about lizards. Riley was glad to see that Jasmine wasn't one of them.

Jasmine turned back to her movie. Riley watched her as she worked. He wanted to keep talking with her. Before he knew it, he was opening his mouth . . .

"I can make some green-screen effects for your movie," Riley offered. "I mean, if you want."

Jasmine stopped what she was doing and turned to Riley.

"Really?"

"Sure." Riley tried to sound casual. Meanwhile, alarm bells were going off in his head. *You don't even have time for your own scene. DON'T HELP THE COMPETITION!!*

Jasmine looked thoughtfully at her project. "Could you make snow — like *falling* snow? And put it over a scene that's already been filmed?"

"Snow?" Riley thought about it. "Oh, sure. I wouldn't even need a green screen. I could just make a digital effect and plop it right into your video."

"It's that easy? Then maybe I could just do it myself at school —"

"NO!" Riley shouted. "I mean, you *might* be able to do it. If you had the right stuff. But sometimes the software and graphics here are kind of . . ." Riley was desperate.

"Super boring?" Jasmine said, completing his thought. "Like the music Mr. Kim showed us?"

"Exactly. So if you want something really awesome, I should do it for you at home." *Really awesome?* Riley wondered at his own words. *Just what exactly are you promising?*

"Okay, great!" said Jasmine. "I'm thinking that the snow would start falling right about here." She showed Riley some of her video. She described how she pictured the effects working with her scene. Riley bobbed his head up and down, saying "sure" to everything. He copied her video onto his flash drive.

"Thanks for helping, Riley," Jasmine said

with a wide smile. "I bet it will look amazing."

Suddenly, Riley wanted to create digital snow so real it could give you frostbite.

On the ride home from school, Riley wrote in his movie notebook. The bouncing SUV made his printing come out wiggly. But he kept writing anyway. He had tons of ideas for Jasmine's digital snow effects, and he didn't want to forget a single one.

Snow Effects for Jasmine's
"MONSTER LOVE STORY" Movie

* Start with a couple of digital snowflakes falling from the sky (as soon as Alfonzo the half-Pegasus dude kicks the bucket).
* Add more snowflakes as the human girl starts to sob like a baby. Make the "wind" blow them in different directions (to add DRAMA).

"Ha!' said Kennedy. "Dahlia — look. It's the video Cam told us about." Kennedy and her BFF Dahlia were sitting beside Riley. Soon, both girls were cackling at a clip on Kennedy's phone.

"What's so funny?" Riley asked.

"Nothing. It's just Leon Courage *totally* flipping out at a restaurant," said Kennedy.

"It's going viral," added Dahlia.

Riley leaned over and squinted at the shaky image on the phone's little screen. Someone had secretly filmed Leon Courage yelling at a waiter. Apparently, the server had put ice in Leon's soft drink by mistake.

"Oh my gosh — Leon just chucked his cup on the ground!" said Dahlia. "The drink *totally* splashed all over that guy serving him!"

"That poor server," said Riley's mom from the driver's seat.

"He soaked the waiter!" said Kennedy. "What a *jerk*."

"I thought you both wanted to marry him," Riley teased.

"Ew — *no thanks*!" Kennedy said.

Kennedy and Dahlia had cooled *waaaay* down over Leon Courage. The singer had tweeted to his fans that he'd be at the mall to sign autographs and pose for pictures. There was even a chance to win backstage passes to his big concert. Of course, Kennedy and Dahlia had gone to the mall first thing in the morning. They'd waited for hours and hours, but Leon Courage never showed up.

"This already has more views than his last music video," Kennedy said, looking at her phone.

"*Ooh* — find that new T.J. Laroche song!" said Dahlia.

T.J. Laroche was their new celebrity crush. Riley yanked his toque over his ears as the girls sang along to the chorus of his awful love song.

Girls are suckers for anything romantic!

Riley turned back to his list and added one more idea for Jasmine's scene:

* Turn some of the snowflakes green to match Alfonzo's "gorgeous" green eyes (Romantic AND Tragic)

#12
Director's Cut

Riley was in his living room. He was lying on his stomach at work on the laptop. It was his fifth try at getting everything just right for Jasmine's movie scene.

Riley clicked play to watch the scene one last time with the digital snow effects he'd made. (He had to admit that even though the story was really romantic and girly, Jasmine and her friends had created amazing claymation. They must have spent *forever* designing the detailed clay characters.)

Finally! Riley thought to himself as the clip ended. The magical, twinkly snow effect was not Riley's usual style, but he'd done a good job. *Now — time to get back to Lizard Beast.* He sat up straight, rearranged the computer onto his lap and did a few neck rolls to loosen up.

Then he spotted the time.

"*WHAT?!?*" Riley said out loud. He'd spent almost *two hours* on Jasmine's magical, twinkling snow! How could he have been so dumb? Tonight was his one chance to make improvements before the sneak preview. The next night, the Fosters were having a huge family party for Riley's grandma's birthday. And Mr. Kim had warned everyone there wouldn't be much more movie time at school.

Frantic, Riley clicked on the new scene he planned to show the class. It was the showdown between Lizard Beast and the mutant horses at the watering hole.

"Please, please, please . . ." Riley muttered. He was wishing his video were somehow much better and more complete than he knew it was. Soon his parents and Kennedy would finish watching their movie downstairs. It would be time for Riley to pack it in for the night. But his scene still needed editing, more special effects, another shot or two of Slow-Mo as Lizard Beast, and . . . *sound!*

Riley slapped himself on the forehead. He'd focused all his attention on getting the visuals right. But he had completely forgotten the audio. Without sound effects — roaring, stomping, snorting — *something* — the big battle scene would be garbage. Without epic sound and music, who would ever believe that Riley's movie was Best Picture material?

Music? No problem! thought Riley quickly. He'd just grab a snippet of action music from the soundtrack samples that came with his software. It might not be perfect — certainly not as good as an original score. But it would have to do.

Unfortunately, the sample sound effects were really crummy.

Think, think, think . . . What should I do for this scene? Finn always made sound effects with everyday objects from around the house. *What would Finn use?*

Riley jumped off the couch and began to tear around the living room. Then the kitchen. Then even the bathroom. He collected random objects that would (hopefully) help him make stunning sound effects. He played the showdown scene in his head as he hunted for props. *Creatures battling on rocky ground, mutant ponies flapping their wings, Lizard Beast roaring . . .* He returned to the living room and dumped the weird collection of things onto the floor. There was a box of his mom's crunchy organic oat cereal for the rocky ground. His dad's electric shaver was for the flapping wings (more of

a buzzing sound, but at this point, *whatever!*).
A hand-held vacuum cleaner would be Lizard
Beast's vicious roar . . .

CRUSH!
WHIRL!
BUZZ!
SQUEAL!

Riley captured the sounds with his laptop's
built-in microphone. As he did, he noticed that
Slow-Mo had started shuffling and scuttling
around like mad in his vivarium. *I need to record
that!* Riley thought. It would be perfect for the
epic battle. He dove for the digital camera on the
coffee table, accidentally sending zombie action
figures, mutant horses and the open cereal box
tumbling to the floor.

And in all the chaos, Riley didn't hear the
door to the basement open.

"THAT'S MY *STUFF!*" Kennedy roared as
she tore into the living room. She scooped up
several of her defaced Magic Rainbow Riders
from the floor. She stared at them in horror.
"What did you do to them?"

"Shh — I'm recording!" shouted Riley.

"I don't care! How could you do this to my things?" Kennedy stepped toward Riley, grinding oat clusters into the beige carpet under her feet. Riley thought he'd seen Kennedy's angriest face when he'd dumped her special shampoo. But now her mouth was twisting in all directions. Her eyes were glowing with anger.

"But you don't use them anymore," Riley protested.

"THEY'RE MINE!"

"What is going on up here?" Riley's parents emerged from the basement.

"Look," Kennedy held out one of her zombified Rainbow Riders.

"Riley!" cried his mom. "What were you thinking?" Then her eyes fell on the carpet. "Is that my cereal all over the floor?"

"I just vacuumed in here!" bellowed Riley's dad.

"I was doing sound effects. Kennedy's the one

who crushed the cereal —"

"I don't want to hear it," Riley's dad cut in. "This is *your* mess. *You* are going to clean it up."

"But I have to finish my scene!"

"No way. You're done with the laptop."

Riley felt his panic surge into overdrive. *Uh-oh. Sneak preview.*

"For how long?" Riley dared to ask.

"Forever!" Kennedy suggested.

"Certainly for right now," Riley's mom answered.

"But it's not fair! Kennedy doesn't ever play with these anymore."

"You know that's not the point," said his dad.

"The point is that all he ever thinks about is his *dumb lizard movie*. He gets in everyone's way and wrecks everyone's stuff . . ." Kennedy took another look at the ponies in her hands, then threw them at Riley's feet. Several pairs of evil mutant horse eyes stared up at Riley from the floor.

"Kennedy — go cool down in your

room," said Riley's mom. "*Now*."

Kennedy crossed her arms and looked straight at Riley. Her eyes were shining, with anger or tears. Maybe both. "You'll do *anything* if it gets you attention!" she shouted. "Even ruining things for other people!" Kennedy turned, stomped out of the living room and slammed her bedroom door.

Riley noticed that he was holding his breath. His mom was shaking her head.

His dad gestured to the organic cereal disaster on the floor. "Good thing you brought out the vacuum," he said, gesturing to Riley. "Get to it."

Sneak-Preview Scene TO-DO List

* Lizard Beast is at his watering hole slurping up water (must add slurping sounds).
* Mutant horses crash out of the bushes and crunch on the gravel ground (add crashing sounds and crunching. Pixels still showing around the tails – fix this!)

* Horses swoop down from the sky (You can still see the strings they're hanging from — BLUR THESE OUT!! Add flapping wing sounds.)
* Add Lizard Beast roar (Find lion roar sound at school? Or a bear? Or a cartoon dinosaur roar?)
* Rocket enters doing ninja kicks (looks more like tap dancing -- fix that up).
* Add action-packed original soundtrack? (too late)

EPIC MOVIE DISASTER!! :(

#13
sneak(y) preview

Riley rushed through the last few sentences in his book journal. Anyone who finished Language Arts early was allowed to use the computers for the last minutes of the school day. With his laptop off limits, this was Riley's final chance to find decent audio before the next day's sneak preview.

Riley was already scanning for a free computer as he scribbled out his last word. Every machine was in use. Even Finn was at a computer!

Riley was suddenly outraged. What could Finn possibly be working on? He'd bailed on *Lizard Beast*. Why should Finn get to have one of the computers? Riley pushed his chair back and marched toward his former friend. He'd get Finn's laptop. He'd threaten to tell Mr. Kim that Finn hadn't done any work in more than a week!

But Finn had left by the time Riley arrived. *Lucky for him*, Riley thought. He shoved in his flash drive and pulled up his soundless show-down scene. As he did, he noticed that the laptop's trash folder was still open. It wasn't empty. Riley took a peek. A file called STUFF had just been moved there. Could this be Finn's secret project?

Riley put on the headphones that were attached to the computer. He threw a glance over his shoulder and angled the laptop screen toward himself. He double-clicked on STUFF.

Soon, Riley was watching the most ridicu-lous video he'd ever seen.

There on screen was Finn. He was standing as still as a statue in his apartment living room. He was dressed in the dumb, pinned-back black sweatpants and the goofy untied glitter sneakers he'd worn to the hockey game. He wore a black tank top showing off his (zero) arm muscles. His hair was slicked up into a pouf, and he had mirrored sunglasses on. No doubt about it, Finn was once again posing as Leon Courage — this time without a trace of zombie makeup. *This has to be a joke*, Riley thought.

In the background, music began to play. It sounded like Finn had recorded the tune on Riley's keyboard. Riley knew for sure when he heard the frosty stardust sound Finn loved to use. An electronic drum beat out a funky dance rhythm, and suddenly Finn sprang to life. Soon he was dancing his heart out, Leon Courage–style. It wasn't his goofy dance with spaghetti arms and twisting hips. In fact, Finn didn't look like he was having any fun at all. His eyes were squinted shut like he was having gas pains. He was jumping around as though the floor was on fire. Every now and

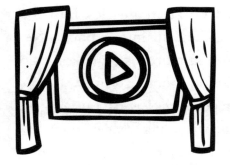

then, he clutched his fists together and pounded them on his chest, like his heart was beating out of control. Every move was timed perfectly to the music, like he'd practised recording himself a thousand times before.

Next came the lyrics:

> *Oh-oh myyyy Jazzz-mine!*
> *Don't say that*
> *Our love only*
> *has-been!*
> *Oh-oh Plea-Yee-Yee-Yeese*
> *Let me win back your heart . . .*

All of a sudden, Riley knew this was not a joke. This was an original Finn Sawchuk production. It was a begging, pleading, syrupy dance number to "win back" Jasmine Santos!

"Wrap it up, folks," Mr. Kim called out. "The bell's going to ring in two minutes."

What was Finn planning to do with this mess? There was no way it was meant for the whole class to watch.

Could Finn be planning to show it to Jasmine in private?

Riley was about to shut down the computer, but stopped. He copied STUFF to his flash drive, then emptied the trash folder.

An idea had sparked in his brain.

The spark grew into a fire on the ride home from school.

It was blazing a few hours later when his mom brought out the cake at his grandma's birthday party.

As Riley drifted off to sleep that night, his idea played out in his brain like it was a scene from a movie.

My Best Friend is a Viral Dancing Zombie

Students sit on the floor in a grade five classroom. Riley Foster, a talented, handsome guy with a great smile, hands Mr. Kim his flash drive. Mr. Kim plugs it into the computer.

MR. KIM: I'm so excited for this, Riley. I'm sure *your* sneak-preview scene will be brilliant. Here we go!

Mr. Kim presses play, and everyone gasps as they stare at the whiteboard. It isn't Riley's movie masterpiece — it's Finn Sawchuk dancing and singing like a dorky Leon Courage. The audience is stunned at the epic fail performance!
Riley looks as shocked as everyone else.

RILEY: How did that get on there?

Finn's face is red. He runs out of the room.

RILEY: Boy, I sure hope this doesn't go viral!

"What a loser," giggled Kennedy to Dahlia. The girls were bent over Kennedy's phone. Riley tried to squirm into a more comfortable position. He couldn't stand it when his dad gave Dahlia a ride to school. It made the back seat squishy. Riley thought he might overheat in his big parka.

"Totally. He thinks he's so hot," said Dahlia.

Ugh — don't say "hot," Riley thought. Then his stomach did a flip. *They couldn't be looking at . . . ?* He glanced quickly at Kennedy's phone, then sighed in relief. It was just another video of Leon Courage behaving badly. Of course, Kennedy wasn't looking at Finn's dance. Why would that be on her phone? And even if it was, what was Riley so worried about? Wasn't that his big plan — to make Finn's dorky dance go viral?

Riley thought of the orange flash drive in his backpack. He tried to enjoy his secret plan like he had the night before. But he was feeling too warm and clammy.

The car lurched as Riley's dad pulled up

to Kennedy's school. Riley's stomach flipped again. "He is SO over," Riley heard Kennedy say to Dahlia as the girls got out of the car. His stomach groaned.

Riley's innards were queasy the whole morning, right through first recess. It wasn't just the hot, bumpy car ride. Riley's breakfast churned the most whenever he thought of the flash drive. He hadn't even done anything with it yet. But he felt like he was going to be sick. Partly, it was because he knew he'd get in trouble with Mr. Kim. There was no good reason for Riley to "accidentally" have Finn's private video.

Second, showing Finn's dumb dance would do nothing to make Riley's crummy, soundless, half-finished sneak-preview scene any better. (That is, if Mr. Kim ever let Riley show videos to the class again!)

And last of all, Riley knew that if he showed the dance, his friendship with Finn would be as over as Leon Courage.

"All right, people," announced Mr. Kim halfway through Science. "Many of you have been *begging* for extra movie time. I'll give you the rest of the period to get your sneak previews ready for this afternoon."

A big *YES!* erupted from the class.

"*Last minute tweaks only!* Don't be afraid to show something that's not quite perfect. Remember — the sneak preview is about getting feedback and making things better."

Riley thought of his plan to show Finn's STUFF video. It was the exact opposite of making anything better. He decided he wouldn't go through with it. He couldn't! He had to delete STUFF off his flash drive right away. He scuttled to a laptop and put on the headphones. He browsed to STUFF, and was about to click delete.

What happened next was never clear to Riley, even in his own brain. It really might have been an accident.

Or maybe, somewhere deep inside, Riley wanted his own last sneak peek at Finn's ridiculous dance. Somehow, Riley found himself clicking play . . .

"What is *that*?" Riley spun around in his chair, twisting his body to hide the screen. He came face to face with Paulo.

"Is that Finn?" Paulo nudged Riley out of his chair. He helped himself to the headphones. "He's not really singing, is he?"

"Shh!" Riley swiped at the headphones, trying to tear them off Paulo's ears. Paulo dodged him every time.

"He *is* singing," Paulo said with a mocking laugh. "This is awesome!"

"I know, I know, but *shhhh*." Riley looked around with a pounding heart. He managed to pull one of the headphones off Paulo's ear. He quickly whispered into that ear: "Mr. Kim will make us stop . . ."

Paulo, still laughing, nodded.

"Vijay!" Paulo said. "Check this out."

Soon Vijay was watching Finn's video beside Paulo. They took turns with the headphones so they could hear the singing. Next Navdeep wandered over. Then Josh. Then Ella . . .

Their whispered comments flew back and forth:

"He's singing like a girl!"

"Or like he got his fingers caught in the door."

"This song's about Jasmine!"

"No way. Wait — oh, man. YOU'RE RIGHT!"

The little group laughed themselves silly over the video. They played it again and again. Riley reached out his hand to turn it off or to rip his drive from the computer. But Paulo kept flicking him away.

"Riley," called Mr. Kim from his desk. "Can I see you a minute?"

Oh, no — Riley was busted. Mr. Kim was going to ask him what all the goofing around was about. What could he say? The evidence was on a bright orange flash drive with the name RILEY FOSTER written in ALL CAPS permanent marker!

"Is that yours?" Mr. Kim asked as Riley approached. *Totally busted*, Riley thought. But when he looked up, he saw that Mr. Kim was pointing to a science assignment on his desk.

"It looks like your printing. But I don't see a name."

"*Ahhhh . . .*" Riley let out a massive sigh of relief. Mr. Kim raised an eyebrow. "I mean, *ahhhh*, no! That's not mine. It might be Ella's. She and I have kind of the same printing. This one's mine." Riley pointed to another sheet without a name.

"Hmm," said Mr. Kim. He quickly scrawled "Ella" and "Riley" on the right pages. "Next time write your name, okay?"

"Yes! Absolutely!" said Riley.

"All right folks, almost lunch," Mr. Kim called out.

With his heart still beating in his throat,

Riley rushed back to the laptop. He noticed that the group was bigger than before . . .

Riley came to a dead stop.

Among the crowd was Finn.

#14
ultimate epic showdown

Other POSSIBLE Scenes for Sneak Preview (?)
* Rocket and Flapjack reading map with Lizard Beast (BLOOPER ENDING hasn't been fixed.)
* Flapjack mixing up zombie virus potion (Crummy animation. Looks like he's cooking!)
* Epic zombie chase scene (NO SOUND. CRUMMY ANIMATION.)
* Pink Pony turning into Mutant Zombie Pony (CRUMMY ANIMATION. NO COLLABORATION. TERRIBLE!!)

"Heads up!" Vijay shouted. Paulo's red ball slammed into the school's brick wall just above Riley's head.

Riley tensed his shoulders and drew his head deeper into his parka. He was sitting on the cold pavement with his back against the wall. His movie notebook was propped up on his lap. Partly, he was still trying to make a decision about what to show at the sneak preview. But mostly he was trying to avoid Finn.

Finn had actually made it pretty easy. He'd taken off as soon as the lunch bell rang. No one had seen him since. Still, Riley chose to hang out near the Paulo-ball boys, even if it meant taking a ball right in the face. He knew Finn would stay away from them at all costs.

But as Vijay retrieved the ball to begin another round, Riley heard him yell, "Hey — over there. *It's Leon Courage!*" Riley's gaze followed Vijay's outstretched arm. Finn, alone and with his head down, was wandering by the portable classroom.

Paulo didn't waste a second. He clutched at his heart and launched into Finn's love song at the top of his lungs: "*Oh, Jazzz-mine! Don't say that our love only has-been!*" Vijay caught on instantly. He tossed the ball aside and busted out a set of jerky hip-hop dance moves. Josh and Navdeep joined in on the clownish dance and crooned along with the others in high, girlish voices: "*Oo-oo-oo . . . Say we are not through-oo-oo . . .*"

Finn didn't move a muscle, as if the slushy ground beneath him was turning to quicksand. Riley noticed a red flush creeping up Finn's neck just above his jacket collar. Soon it spread all over Finn's face.

Riley stood up and took a step toward Finn. Sure, his video had been an epic fail, but no one deserved this. Not even Finn — the big-shot lucky-charm superstar. Riley cleared his throat, not sure what he was about to say . . .

"HOW DARE YOU!" A furious voice ripped through the air. It was Jasmine. She was stomping toward Finn, Riley and the Paulo-ball dance troupe. She was followed closely by Arusha and Claire.

Jasmine planted herself in front of Finn. She stared him fiercely in the face.

Arusha and Claire stood behind her, their arms crossed like bodyguards.

"Why did you write that stupid song? You made it sound like we were going out," Jasmine hollered. "We were NEVER going out!"

Finn's mouth dropped open. But before he could reply, Paulo and his buddies started singing even louder: "Oo-oo-oo . . . *Please-yee-yee-yeese* . . ."

Jasmine turned on the musical monkeys. "Cut it out!" But her yelling only inspired sillier dance moves.

"Come on, guys," said Riley. "It's not funny."

Jasmine wheeled around to face him. "*You're* one to talk, Riley! Claire said the video was on your flash drive."

"What?" Finn said, suddenly finding his lost voice. He turned his face toward Riley. On it was a look of anger, horror and disbelief mashed up into one. Riley felt his stomach dive toward his sneakers.

"You'd both better stop spreading

lies about me," Jasmine said. "Or . . . I'll *sue* you!"

Vijay fell to the ground, crunched up into a ball and laughed himself silly. Paulo, cackling like a hyena, collapsed down beside his friend.

"Jasmine's mom is a lawyer," said Arusha, sticking out her chin. "She can sue all of you."

"We're *soooo* scared," Navdeep said between gasps for air. Jasmine rolled her eyes, whirled around and stormed off with her loyal bodyguards.

The Paulo-ball guys continued hooting and making fun. Finn took a step toward Riley.

"*You* showed it?" Finn asked.

Riley shrugged. He couldn't exactly deny it.

"How did you get it, anyway?" Finn took  another step closer. "Did you steal it?"

Riley scoffed. "I didn't *steal*. You left it open on the computer yesterday — anyone could have seen it."

"But *you* showed it,"

Finn said. He gave Riley's shoulder a sharp shove.

Riley glanced down at his shoulder, as if Finn's fingers had burned a hole in his parka. Why should Finn push *him* around? He'd been feeling bad all morning, and he hadn't even gone through with his plan! *He* wasn't the one laughing and rolling on the ground. He had tried to put a stop to the taunting.

So Riley retorted: "Why would *you* make a video like that? And bring it to school?" He raised his arms and returned Finn's shove. "That was pretty stupid."

"It was none of your business!" This time Finn pushed Riley so hard he almost toppled over.

"None of my business?" Riley shot back. "That's a joke, right? I thought everything you did was *everyone's* business."

"*You're* the one obsessed with getting attention," Finn retorted.

"Not for dancing like Leon Courage."

At first, Finn's eyes went wide with rage.

Then his expression changed to a smirk. He mumbled something under his breath.

Riley took a step closer. He and Finn were nose to nose. "What did you just say?" He grabbed Finn's collar with his left hand. He felt the fingers on his right hand twitch.

"I said . . . *you're jealous*," said Finn. "That's why you're being such a jerk."

"*Me* jealous of *you*?" Riley gave Finn's collar a shake. "For what?"

Finn was breathing hard. His freckled face was splotched red and pink. "*Your* name didn't get on the news. *Your* name didn't get on a podcast. So you showed my video *for revenge*!"

"I didn't show it! Paulo saw it by mistake," Riley said through gritted teeth, their noses almost touching.

"You're the one who wants to get famous," Finn said. "You're just mad it happened to *me*!"

Riley could feel Paulo and his crew, now up on their feet, closing in on them. Watching, waiting.

"Are they going to fight?" he heard Paulo say.

Riley and Finn wheeled in a dizzying circle,

holding each other in a tight grip. They lunged and pulled. They were like two bucks proving their strength, their arms locked together like antlers.

Finn planted his feet on the ground and gave Riley one last, hard push. Riley found himself landed on the cold, hard pavement. Riley felt stunned, in his body and in his brain.

"You'll do anything for attention!" Finn shouted down at Riley from where he stood over him. *"Even if it means crushing your friends."*

The other boys were hooting and jeering, urging a fight.

For a moment, anything could have happened. It looked as though Finn was really going to crush Riley.

Then the bell rang.

Finn turned and ran toward the school, leaving Riley alone on the pavement.

#15
FeedbaCK

"Next, we have a scene from *Alfonzo of Windworld*," said Mr. Kim, looking at his list. "Ready, girls?"

Jasmine nodded. Riley noticed that she was sitting up front close to Mr. Kim — as far away as she could from him and from Finn. He and Finn were at the back, but on opposite corners of the carpet. It might as well have been opposite sides of the ocean.

Riley was trying hard to forget what had happened at lunchtime and to concentrate on the sneak preview. But each time Mr. Kim showed a clip on the whiteboard, Riley remembered that his own turn would be after recess. He only had a few minutes left to enjoy being known as the classroom's best movie-maker.

As Jasmine's scene began, the whole class let out a soft "Ooooooo . . ." Even Riley, who had watched this scene about a million times on his home laptop, was impressed. The video looked so crisp and clear up on the big screen.

"*Wake up, my dear, sweet Alfonzo*," said Josephina, the clay character with the long black hair. The little figure knelt beside the half-Pegasus dude. He lay on the ground as his hooves twitched in agony.

Riley found himself leaning forward and listening carefully. The girls hadn't yet added the sound when Riley first saw it. There was a music soundtrack, too. It was a soft, slow tune with high, sad-sounding notes. Funny how the right movie music could make you feel happy, scared or sad.

Josephina leaned close to Alfonzo's face. His eyelids became droopier and droopier, covering his bright green eyes. The sad music got louder.

Where have I heard this song before? Riley wondered. *Is it from a movie? It sounds familiar.*

Then, a chiming, twinkling breezy sound rose above the rest of the music. Riley knew it right away. It was the stardust sound from his very own keyboard, Finn's favourite musical effect.

Riley whipped his gaze across the room and locked eyes with Finn. He raised his eyebrows, amazed. He didn't know Finn made the music for *this* scene — or that his friend *could* make something that sounded so amazing (so "romantic and tragic"!).

"Oh no!" someone in the class gasped. Riley turned his attention back to Jasmine's video. On screen, Alfonzo's hooves had stopped twitching and his eyes closed for good. Then, from the top left-hand corner of the screen, one of Riley's swirling, twinkling digital snowflakes trailed down into the scene. Snowflake followed snowflake, including bright green ones the colour of Alfonzo's "gorgeous" eyes. "*Ooooooo . . .*" everyone said again.

But what amazed Riley most was this: As the digital snowstorm increased, Finn's stardust music became more intense. The snow danced and fell and tumbled in perfect rhythm with Finn's silvery keyboard music. They hadn't planned it. They hadn't even known they were working on the same scene! But somehow Finn's music and Riley's digital effects looked like they were made for each other . . .

THE END came up on the screen, and the credits rolled:

Written and Directed by Jasmine, Arusha and Claire

Clay Characters by Claire

Set and Voices by Arusha

Edited by Jasmine

A special thanks to Finn (Music) and Riley (Extra Special Effects)

Riley couldn't help himself. Once again, he looked across the room and caught Finn's eye.

"So . . . that was pretty neat," said Riley. He and Finn were standing near the coat hooks, putting on their parkas for recess. "I mean, how our music and effects went together in Jasmine's movie. And . . . *stuff*."

"Yeah," said Finn in a quiet voice. "It was . . . kind of cool."

Riley looked up at the ceiling, then back at Finn. "*Sooooo* . . ." he said. "What should we do?"

"What do you mean?" Finn asked.

"It's our sneak-preview turn after recess," said Riley. "Is there anything we can show?"

Finn shrugged. "How should I know?" His voice sounded bitter.

Riley felt a flicker of anger. "Hey — you ditched *Lizard Beast*, remember?"

"You were ignoring me," said Finn, his voice rising. "And you always take over, anyway."

"Well, you always fool around!" said Riley.

"That's 'cause there's never anything for me to do," Finn retorted. "All the fancy equipment is yours."

Riley bit his lip. He knew they could keep arguing forever. They could bat hurtful things back and forth like a ping-pong match. But what was the point?

"You know," Riley said slowly. "Sometimes your fooling around stuff isn't too bad. Remember the deleted scenes?"

Finn relaxed his shoulders a bit. "Yeah," he said. "Those were fun."

"We actually got some pretty good footage," Riley said. An idea was beginning to spark. "For one thing, those scenes have sound. Some have your keyboard music."

"Some of your special effects were pretty sweet," Finn admitted. "But . . . it's just us fooling around. There's no story."

"I don't know, Finn. We have our characters figured out.

And most of the scenes had a script. Maybe we just need a way to tie it together."

Riley watched as Finn got a thoughtful look on his face.

"I guess at least we did the deleted scenes together," Finn said.

"Right," Riley agreed. "Mr. Kim is big on collaboration. So?" He held up his movie notebook. "Want to figure something out?"

"Okay," said Finn.

There was an awkward pause. Riley was sure that if the moment had been in a movie, they'd be hearing crickets in the background.

"Uh . . . we're not going to hug, are we?" Finn finally asked.

"Nope," said Riley.

"Good. Then let's work on that idea."

NEW IDEA
(an underpaid!)
"Confessions of a ⌃ Reptile Action Star"
A (Very) Original Movie
by Riley and Finn

The (NEW) Main Movie Idea:

A lizard actor named Slow-Mo gets hired to be in a new epic action movie. Lizard Beast versus the Zombie Horde. But the movie and everything about it STINKS! Props keep falling over. Things go wrong on the set all the time. And the actors who play Rocket and Flapjack are always worrying about their beards and goofing around.

Slow-Mo films all the behind-the-scenes bloopers and movie-set disasters with his hidden camera. And decides to share the footage with the world!

#16
hidden camera movie magic

Riley and Finn's best deleted scenes were about to play for the class. The friends sat side by side on the carpet. Finn was fidgeting. Riley sat as still as a statue. *Will anyone think it's good?* Riley thought. *Will they laugh?*

The first scene lit up the whiteboard with animated action:

Rocket. Flapjack and Lizard Beast run toward a cave to hide from the zombies. Something flies out at them. It looks like a colony of bats. but it's a flock of Riley's flying digital moustaches! (Finn's creepy flapping-wings sound effect fills the air.)

The entire class burst out laughing as they watched the silly scene. Riley felt himself relax just a bit.

LIZARD BEAST: This is bad. We've disturbed the Possessed Facial Hair!

There were more laughs from the audience when Slow-Mo "spoke." It wasn't just Finn's crazy lizard voice. Slow-Mo seemed to suddenly grow a pair of human lips. (Riley had made a video of Finn's talking mouth, then added the cut-out talking lips onto Slow-Mo's face.)

Finn poked Riley and pointed to Paulo and Vijay. The two boys were chuckling as they watched. Vijay was even balancing a pencil between his nose and upper lip, pretending it was a moustache.

"I think we're rockin' it!" Finn whispered as the next clip began to roll.

Flapjack. Rocket and Lizard Beast are standing around. doing nothing.

FLAPJACK: Come on. Rocket. Show us your sweetest moves.

Finn's keyboard dance music starts up. Suddenly. all the characters have digital Leon Courage hairdos.

"That's so *random*!" Riley overheard Ella say as she giggled.

Rocket moves his action-figure body awkwardly to the music.

ROCKET: How's this?

FLAPJACK: Ick. Terrible. Let Mr. Flapjack show YOU how to par-TAY.

Flapjack busts a few jerky dance moves of his own.

LIZARD BEAST: That's nothing. I'm going to take you BOTH to dance school.

Lizard Beast. in perfect time with the music. is suddenly doing amazing hip-hop gestures with his front legs.

The class howled at the scene, loving the crazy voices and animated effects. Riley even noticed Jasmine lean toward Arusha and Claire and say, "He's *sooooo* cute." (He liked hearing that, even though he knew she was talking about Slow-Mo!)

"Rockin' it!" Finn said again, giving Riley another poke in the arm. Riley nodded. It had been a while since he'd watched some of these scenes. They were good — *really* good.

Of course, Riley knew there was no way they'd get Best Picture now. Even he could see that Jasmine and her friends deserved that award. But once he and Finn added in Slow-Mo as the movie-star narrator, they'd have something pretty special. Maybe they'd win the award for Most Hilarious — although Navdeep and Josh's movie with the animated talking sandwich would probably get that one. Or possibly Most Original? That didn't sound bad . . .

"This is a good start, guys," Mr. Kim told Riley and Finn after the whole class had applauded for their clips. "Very careful animation. Some excellent music and sound effects. And I can see both of your personalities coming through in the Rocket and Flapjack characters."

Riley and Finn exchanged a look. Finn was wearing a wide, goofy grin. Riley's own face was tight from smiling. They'd survived the sneak preview!

"But," Mr. Kim continued. "For the final edit, I *would* like to see you two make your main movie idea more clear to pull it all together. Think you can do that?"

"That's our plan," said Finn.

"No problem," Riley agreed. "We've got this!"

Riley and Finn climbed into the Foster SUV after school. Kennedy was already there, with her nose to her phone as usual.

"So where do you think Slow-Mo should keep his hidden camera?" Riley asked.

"In his armpit?" Finn suggested.

Riley took a pencil out of his pocket and spread the movie notebook between them as they settled into the back seat.

"I like it," said Riley. "But it might be kind of hard to animate."

"How about in a big hat," said Finn. "Like a sombrero?" "Yes!" Riley jotted down the idea. "Definitely a sombrero."

"*Awwwwww*," Kennedy cooed out loud. "He's *soooo* sweet!"

Riley and Finn glanced over at Kennedy's phone. On screen was a video of Leon Courage. The pop star was dressed in normal-looking jeans and a normal-looking T-shirt for once (although his hair was still styled in a slick pouf).

He held a bucket and stood near a sign that said "Sally's Animal Rescue Farm." He was tossing food from the bucket to a bunch of baby goats.

"I thought you said Leon Courage was a big jerk," Riley said.

"Leon's different now," Kennedy said. "He tweeted out to all his fans that he's *super* sorry. He's been under a lot of pressure with his big concert tour and his new album."

Riley snickered as Finn pretended to gag. Kennedy, still looking at the video, sighed. "Leon says he just wants to 'give back.'"

"To the goats?" Finn asked. Riley snorted.

Kennedy glared at the boys. "People can *change*!" she huffed.

"Yeah," Finn whispered to Riley, "change into Goat Dude!"

"All he needs is a manly goat beard," Riley whispered back.

The boys shared a chuckle and got back to work on their new script.

Riley's Movie Talk

Alpha channel — Something that lets you make parts of a video invisible. That way, you can layer your video onto another one and make them blend together. (Using this term will really impress other movie-makers!)

Animation — A movie style where still pictures are put together to make it look like things are moving. (Takes a very long time to do!)

Audio — Another word for **sound**. In movies, it's stuff like characters talking, soundtrack music and sound effects.

Blockbuster — An epic, amazing movie with lots of action. A HUGE hit!

Blooper — When something goes wrong during filming, like when an actor messes up his lines (or when his fake moustache falls off...)

Credits — A long list of ALLLLLLL the people who helped make the movie, like the actors, the director and the writers . . . even the people who serve everyone sandwiches on the movie set.

Deleted scenes — Parts of the movie that get cut out of the final version, like bloopers. Sometimes deleted scenes are run during the credits to make the audience laugh.

Footage — Another name for the video you record with your camera (has nothing to do with your foot ☺).

Green screen — A neon green screen* you use as a background. Later you can remove all the green colour, leaving only the action, which you can put on top of a different scene or background. *Bright green is used because not a lot of things are that colour. When you remove the green, you aren't removing parts of the thing you're filming.*

Live action — A video recording of something that really happened, like a pet lizard walking across your living room (or your friend waving an action figure around and giving it a funny voice).

Movie notebook — A place to keep all your movie ideas so you don't forget anything.

Post production — Anything that happens after you take your video footage (like adding crazy digital hairdos for your pet lizard).

Shoot — To take a picture or record a video.

Soundtrack — The music that plays in the background during a movie. It can make you feel sad, scared, happy or excited. Make sure the music matches the mood of the scene.

Special effects — Interesting details you add to your video to make it more exciting. Some special effects are sounds, like crunchy footsteps on a rocky path. Some effects are cool things to look at, like digital snowflakes.

Stop-motion — When you take a bunch of still pictures of something, changing it a little bit every time. Then, when you put the pictures together, it looks like the thing is moving and things are happening (like how a flipbook works).

Storyboard — A plan for what will happen in a movie. Each scene is drawn and laid out in the order the scenes will go. (Some people put their drawings on a big board. BUT, you can use mini sticky notes and a page from your movie notebook so you can take your storyboard to school.)

Tagline — An exciting sentence or two that describes the main idea of your movie. Sometimes you see a tagline on a movie poster. Or sometimes a guy with a really deep voice says the tagline during an ad for the movie.